The Mystique of the Sea: Poems, Stories, and Intriguing Facts

Compiled by Carol Mays

ISBN Number: 9781794256347

To the Primal Spring and all who cherish her infinite manifestations.

Table of Contents

Introduction

The significance of the sea to each person is almost as variable and multi-faceted as the sea itself. It can represent beauty, vastness, wonder, romance, and endless possibilities. Yet, depending upon one's experiences, it can also bring up memories of danger, war, entrapment, pain, or loss. For people living on or near the sea, it is a large part of their daily lives. To others living well inland, it hardly figures at all into their daily routines, and instead represents the dream or the possibility of an escape.

I am one of those who, living well inland, dreams of the beauty, vastness, and wonder of the sea. The last time I visited it, I so cherished the experience that I decided to put together a book which expressed these feelings, for the benefit of myself and others. Even though, as a poet and author, I had not written much on this subject, I figured it would be fairly easy to find literature in the public domain and intriguing facts from various sources that I could use.

I was surprised to find out that there was a great discrepancy, in terms of emotional tone, between sea stories and sea poems. I had to search far and wide for sea stories that were readily readable in today's English and were not drenched in horror, violence, and inhumanity. Arthur Conan Doyle came to my rescue with two stories—suspenseful, but not vile and violent. Then I included part of the official British Titanic investigation report, out of sheer interest, and a highly entertaining classic Russian story. Sadly, these latter also include their own form of a somewhat more civilized inhumanity.

I came across some poems that expressed visions of horror, but usually sea-related poems were more subtle and romantic than the hard-hitting and often difficult-to-decipher stories. I chose poems that I thought were expansive and nurtured the soul and the imagination. My favorite poet, Edgar Allan Poe, was included because he was a master at creating deeply imaginative, otherworldly scenes. I searched through a few poetry books, but mostly I found multiple listings for poems online, through sites such as Poem Hunter.com, Poetry Foundation.org, and Poetry Archive.org.

Facts were plentiful and fascinating—sometimes delightful and inspiring, sometimes frightening and sobering. I included many that I thought were great for broadening one's horizons about our endlessly fascinating and changing world.

I have compiled this book for you—and also for myself. I want to have something stimulating and sea-related to read, the next time I go to the beach, and I know now that finding such a book is not so easy. As for you, I hope you find this to your liking, and bon voyage!

I

Poems

A Wanderer's Song

A wind's in the heart of me, a fire's in my heels,
I am tired of brick and stone and rumbling wagon-
   wheels;
I hunger for the sea's edge, the limit of the land,
Where the wild old Atlantic is shouting on the sand.

Oh I'll be going, leaving the noises of the street,
To where a lifting foresail-foot is yanking at the
   sheet;
To a windy, tossing anchorage where yawls and
   ketches ride,
Oh I'll be going, going, until I meet the tide.

And first I'll hear the sea-wind, the mewing of the
   gulls,
The clucking, sucking of the sea about the rusty
   hulls,
The songs at the capstan at the hooker warping
   out,
And then the heart of me'll know I'm there or
   thereabout.

Oh I am sick of brick and stone, the heart of me is
   sick,
For windy green, unquiet sea, the realm of Moby
   Dick;
And I'll be going, going, from the roaring of the
   wheels,
For a wind's in the heart of me, a fire's in my heels.

                       John Masefield

Annabel Lee

It was many and many a year ago,
   In a kingdom by the sea,
That a maiden there lived whom you may know
   By the name of Annabel Lee;
And this maiden she lived with no other thought
   Than to love and be loved by me.

I was a child and *she* was a child,
   In this kingdom by the sea,
But we loved with a love that was more than love—
   I and my Annabel Lee—
With a love that the wingèd seraphs of heaven
   Coveted her and me.

And this was the reason that, long ago,
   In this kingdom by the sea,
A wind blew out of a cloud, chilling
   My beautiful Annabel Lee;
So that her high-born kinsmen came
   And bore her away from me,
To shut her up in a sepulchre
   In this kingdom by the sea.

The angels, not half so happy in heaven,
   Went envying her and me—
Yes!—that was the reason (as all men know,
   In this kingdom by the sea)
That the wind came out of the cloud by night,
   Chilling and killing my Annabel Lee.

14

But our love it was stronger by far than the love
 Of those who were older than we—
 Of many far wiser than we—
And neither the angels in heaven above
 Nor the demons down under the sea
Can ever dissever my soul from the soul
 Of the beautiful Annabel Lee;

For the moon never beams, without bringing me
 dreams
 Of the beautiful Annabel Lee;
And the stars never rise, but I feel the bright eyes
 Of the beautiful Annabel Lee;
And so, all the night-tide, I lie down by the side
Of my darling—my darling—my life and my bride,

 In her sepulchre there by the sea—
 In her tomb by the sounding sea.

                         Edgar Allan Poe

Cargoes

Quinquireme of Nineveh from distant Ophir,
Rowing home to haven in sunny Palestine,
With a cargo of ivory,
And apes and peacocks,
Sandalwood, cedarwood, and sweet white wine.

Stately Spanish galleon coming from the Isthmus,
Dipping through the Tropics by the palm-green
    shores,
With a cargo of diamonds,
Emeralds, amethysts,
Topazes, and cinnamon, and gold moidores.

Dirty British coaster with a salt-caked smoke-stack,
Butting through the Channel in the mad March
    days,
With a cargo of Tyne coal,
Road-rails, pig-lead,
Firewood, iron-ware, and cheap tin trays.

John Masefield

Dream-Land

By a route obscure and lonely,
Haunted by ill angels only,
Where an Eidolon, named Night,
On a black throne reigns upright,
I have reached these lands but newly
From an ultimate dim Thule—
From a wild weird clime that lieth, sublime,
    Out of Space—Out of Time.

Bottomless vales and boundless floods,
And chasms, and caves, and Titan woods,
With forms that no man can discover
For the dews that drip all over;
Mountains toppling evermore
Into seas without a shore;
Seas that restlessly aspire,
Surging, unto skies of fire;
Lakes that endlessly outspread
Their lone waters—lone and dead,—
Their still waters—still and chilly
With the snows of the lolling lily.

By the lakes that thus outspread
Their lone waters, lone and dead,—
Their sad waters, sad and chilly
With the snows of the lolling lily,—
By the mountains—near the river
Murmuring lowly, murmuring ever,—
By the grey woods,—by the swamp
Where the toad and the newt encamp,—

By the dismal tarns and pools
  Where dwell the Ghouls,—
By each spot the most unholy—
In each nook most melancholy,—
There the traveller meets, aghast,
Sheeted Memories of the Past—
Shrouded forms that start and sigh
As they pass the wanderer by—
White-robed forms of friends long given,
In agony, to the Earth—and Heaven.

For the heart whose woes are legion
'Tis a peaceful, soothing region—
For the spirit that walks in shadow
'Tis—oh, 'tis an Eldorado!
But the traveller, travelling through it,
May not—dare not openly view it;
Never its mysteries are exposed
To the weak human eye unclosed;
So wills its King, who hath forbid
The uplifting of the fring'd lid;
And thus the sad Soul that here passes
Beholds it but through darkened glasses.

By a route obscure and lonely,
Haunted by ill angels only,
Where an Eidolon, named Night,
On a black throne reigns upright,
I have wandered home but newly
From this ultimate dim Thule.

Edgar Allan Poe

Drifting – Poem

My soul to-day
Is far away,
Sailing the Vesuvian Bay;
My winged boat,
A bird afloat,
Swings round the purple peaks remote: --

Round purple peaks
It sails, and seeks
Blue inlets and their crystal creeks,
Where high rocks throw,
Through deeps below,
A duplicated golden glow.

Far, vague, and dim,
The mountains swim;
While on Vesuvius' misty brim,
With outstretched hands,
The gray smoke stands
O'erlooking the volcanic lands.

Here Ischia smiles
O'er liquid miles;
And yonder, bluest of the isles,
Calm Capri waits,
Her sapphire gates
Beguiling to her bright estates.

I heed not, if
My rippling skiff

Float swift or slow from cliff to cliff;
With dreamful eyes
My spirit lies
Under the walls of Paradise.

Under the walls
Where swells and falls
The Bay's deep breast at intervals,
At peace I lie,
Blown softly by,
A cloud upon this liquid sky.

The day, so mild,
Is Heaven's own child,
With Earth and Ocean reconciled;
The airs I feel
Around me steal
Are murmuring to the murmuring keel.

Over the rail
My hand I trail
Within the shadow of the sail,
A joy intense,
The cooling sense
Glides down my drowsy indolence.

With dreamful eyes
My spirit lies
Where Summer sings and never dies, --
O'erveiled with vines
She glows and shines
Among her future oil and wines.

Her children, hid
The cliffs amid,
Are gamboling with the gamboling kid;
Or down the walls,
With tipsy calls,
Laugh on the rocks like waterfalls.

The fisher's child,
With tresses wild,
Unto the smooth, bright sand beguiled,
With glowing lips
Sings as she skips,
Or gazes at the far-off ships.

Yon deep bark goes
Where traffic blows,
From lands of sun to lands of snows; --
This happier one,
Its course is run
From lands of snow to lands of sun.

O happy ship,
To rise and dip,
With the blue crystal at your lip!
O happy crew,
My heart with you
Sails, and sails, and sings anew!

No more, no more
The worldly shore
Upbraids me with its loud uproar!
With dreamful eyes

My spirit lies
Under the walls of Paradise!

Thomas Buchanan Read

Exiled

Searching my heart for its true sorrow,
This is the thing I find to be:
That I am weary of words and people,
Sick of the city, wanting the sea;

Wanting the sticky, salty sweetness
Of the strong wind and shattered spray;
Wanting the loud sound and the soft sound
Of the big surf that breaks all day.

Always before about my dooryard,
Marking the reach of the winter sea,
Rooted in sand and dragging drift-wood,
Straggled the purple wild sweet-pea;

Always I climbed the wave at morning,
Shook the sand from my shoes at night,
That now am caught beneath great buildings,
Stricken with noise, confused with light.

If I could hear the green piles groaning
Under the windy wooden piers,
See once again the bobbing barrels,
And the black sticks that fence the weirs,

If I could see the weedy mussels
Crusting the wrecked and rotting hulls,
Hear once again the hungry crying
Overhead, of the wheeling gulls,

Feel once again the shanty straining
Under the turning of the tide,
Fear once again the rising freshet,
Dread the bell in the fog outside,—

I should be happy,—that was happy
All day long on the coast of Maine!
I have a need to hold and handle
Shells and anchors and ships again!

I should be happy, that am happy
Never at all since I came here.
I am too long away from water.
I have a need of water near.

               Edna St. Vincent Millay

Exultation is the Going

Exultation is the going
Of an inland soul to sea,
Past the houses—past the headlands—
Into deep Eternity—

Bred as we, among the mountains,
Can the sailor understand
The divine intoxication
Of the first league out from land?

Emily Dickinson

Harbor Dawn

There's a hush and stillness calm and deep,
For the waves have wooed all the winds to sleep
In the shadow of headlands bold and steep;
But some gracious spirit has taken the cup
Of the crystal sky and filled it up
With rosy wine, and in it afar
Has dissolved the pearl of the morning star.

The girdling hills with the night-mist cold
In purple raiment are hooded and stoled
And smit on the brows with fire and gold;
And in the distance the wide, white sea
Is a thing of glamor and wizardry,
With its wild heart lulled to a passing rest,
And the sunrise cradled upon its breast.

With the first red sunlight on mast and spar
A ship is sailing beyond the bar,
Bound to a land that is fair and far;
And those who wait and those who go
Are brave and hopeful, for well they know
Fortune and favor the ship shall win
That crosses the bar when the dawn comes in.

Lucy Maud Montgomery

In Port

Out of the fires of the sunset come we again to our
　own
We have girdled the world in our sailing under
　many an orient star;
Still to our battered canvas the scents of the spice
　gales cling,
And our hearts are swelling within us as we cross
　the harbor bar.

Beyond are the dusky hills where the twilight hangs
　in the pine trees,
Below are the lights of home where are watching
　the tender eyes
We have dreamed of on fretted seas in the hours of
　long night-watches,
Ever a beacon to us as we looked to the stranger
　skies.

Hark! how the wind comes out of the haven's arms
　to greet us,
Bringing with it the song that is sung on the ancient
　shore!
Shipmates, furl we our sails we have left the seas
　behind us,
Gladly finding at last our homes and our loves once
　more.

Lucy Maud Montgomery

Long Island Sound

I see it as it looked one afternoon
In August,— by a fresh soft breeze o'erblown.
The swiftness of the tide, the light thereon,
A far-off sail, white as a crescent moon.
The shining waters with pale currents strewn,
The quiet fishing-smacks, the Eastern cove,
The semi-circle of its dark, green grove.
The luminous grasses, and the merry sun
In the grave sky; the sparkle far and wide,
Laughter of unseen children, cheerful chirp
Of crickets, and low lisp of rippling tide,
Light summer clouds fantastical as sleep
Changing unnoted while I gazed thereon.
All these fair sounds and sights I made my own.

Emma Lazarus

Meeting at Night

The gray sea and the long black land;
And the yellow half-moon large and low;
And the startled little waves that leap
In fiery ringlets from their sleep,
As I gain the cove with pushing prow,
And quench its speed i' the slushy sand.

Then a mile of warm sea-scented beach;
Three fields to cross till a farm appears;
A tap at the pane, the quick sharp scratch
And blue spurt of a lighted match,
And a voice less loud, through its joys and
   fears,
Than the two hearts beating each to each!

Robert Browning

My Longshore Lass

Far in the mellow western sky,
Above the restless harbor bar,
A beacon on the coast of night,
Shines out a calm, white evening star;
But your deep eyes, my 'longshore lass,
Are brighter, clearer far.

The glory of the sunset past
Still gleams upon the water there,
But all its splendor cannot match
The wind-blown brightness of your hair;
Not any sea-maid's floating locks
Of gold are half so fair.

The waves are whispering to the sands
With murmurs as of elfin glee;
But your low laughter, 'longshore lass,
Is like a sea-harp's melody,
And the vibrant tones of your tender voice
Are sweeter far to me.

Lucy Maud Montgomery

Newport at Night

City lights sparkling,
mirrored in the Bay,
multi-colored jewels—
amber, rose, and green,
crystal, diamond-white—
gracing bridge and buildings—
mansions, pubs, and shops—
fanciful reflections of
countless points of intrigue.
Neurons, lives entwining—
schemes, ideas, and passions—
complex as a motherboard,
vibrant as a heartbeat,
fertile and entrancing,
as though fashioned by a
cosmic magician's spell.

Carol Mays

Night

A pale enchanted moon is sinking low
Behind the dunes that fringe the shadowy lea,
And there is haunted starlight on the flow
Of immemorial sea.

I am alone and need no more pretend
Laughter or smile to hide a hungry heart;
I walk with solitude as with a friend
Enfolded and apart.

We tread an eerie road across the moor
Where shadows weave upon their ghostly looms,
And winds sing an old lyric that might lure
Sad queens from ancient tombs.

I am a sister to the loveliness
Of cool far hill and long-remembered shore,
Finding in it a sweet forgetfulness
Of all that hurt before.

The world of day, its bitterness and cark,
No longer have the power to make me weep;
I welcome this communion of the dark
As toilers welcome sleep.

Lucy Maud Montgomery

Off to the Fishing Ground

There's a piping wind from a sunrise shore
Blowing over a silver sea,
There's a joyous voice in the lapsing tide
That calls enticingly;
The mist of dawn has taken flight
To the dim horizon's bound,
And with wide sails set and eager hearts
We're off to the fishing ground.

Ho, comrades mine, how that brave wind sings
Like a great sea-harp afar!
We whistle its wild notes back to it
As we cross the harbor bar.
Behind us there are the homes we love
And hearts that are fond and true,
And before us beckons a strong young day
On leagues of glorious blue.

Comrades, a song as the fleet goes out,
A song of the orient sea!
We are the heirs of its tingling strife,
Its courage and liberty.
Sing as the white sails cream and fill,
And the foam in our wake is long,
Sing till the headlands black and grim
Echo us back our song!

Oh, 'tis a glad and heartsome thing
To wake ere the night be done
And steer the course that our fathers steered

In the path of the rising sun.
The wind and welkin and wave are ours
Wherever our bourne is found,
And we envy no landsman his dream and sleep
When we're off to the fishing ground.

Lucy Maud Montgomery

On a Summer Shore

Long years have gone, and yet it seems
    But scarce an hour ago,
I lay upon a moss-grown rock,
    And watched the ebb and flow
Of waters, where cool shades above
    Glassed in cool depths below.
You stood beside me sweet and fair,
    A basket on your arm,
Red-heaped with luscious fruit we'd picked
    Down at the old shore-farm;
You stood and in the shore-wood made
    A picture glad and warm.
Like heaving pearl the blue bay rocked
    Against its limestone wall,
Far off in reeling dreams of blue
    The heavens seemed to fall
About the world, and there you stood,
    Unconscious, queen of all.
From far-off fields the low of kine,
    Soft bird-notes, airy streams,
That stole in here, far, broken notes
    Of all the day's hushed dreams;
And you, one slender shaft of light,
    In all the world's wide gleams.
We spoke no love, for I was shy,
    And you were shyer then;
Mine was a boy's faint heart, and yours
    Still outside of love's ken;
But such sweet moments are full rare
    In barren years of men

And often when the heart is worn
　　And life grows sorrow-wise,
I dream again a blue, north bay,
　　A gleam of summer skies;
And by my side a young girl stands
　　With heaven in her eyes.
You are a dream, a face, a wraith,
　　You drift across my pain,
I lock you in my sacred past
　　Where all love's ghosts remain;
But life hath nought for me so sweet
　　As you can bring again.

William Wilfred Campbell

On the Cliffs, Newport

Tonight a shimmer of gold lies mantled o'er
Smooth lovely Ocean. Through the lustrous gloom
A savor steals from linden trees in bloom
And gardens ranged at many a palace door.
Proud walls rise here, and, where the moonbeams
    pour
Their pale enchantment down the dim coast-line,
Terrace and lawn, trim hedge and flowering vine,
Crown with fair culture all the sounding shore.
How sweet, to such a place, on such a night,
From halls with beauty and festival a-glare,
To come distract and, stretched on the cool turf,
Yield to some fond, improbable delight,
While the moon, reddening, sinks, and all the air
Sighs with the muffled tumult of the surf!

Alan Seeger

Pandora's Songs

. . . As an immortal nightingale
I sing behind the summer sky
Thro' leaves of starlight gold and pale
That shiver with my melody,
Along the wake of the full-moon
Far on to oceans, and beyond
Where the horizons vanish down
In darkness clear as diamond. . .

Trumbull Stickney

Sea Longing

A thousand miles beyond this sun-steeped wall
Somewhere the waves creep cool along the sand,
The ebbing tide forsakes the listless land
With the old murmur, long and musical;
The windy waves mount up and curve and fall,
And round the rocks the foam blows up like snow,--

Tho' I am inland far, I hear and know,
For I was born the sea's eternal thrall.
I would that I were there and over me
The cold insistence of the tide would roll,
Quenching this burning thing men call the soul,--
Then with the ebbing I should drift and be
Less than the smallest shell along the shoal,
Less than the sea-gulls calling to the sea.

Sara Teasdale

Sea Sunset

A gallant city has been builded far
In the pied heaven,
Bannered with crimson, sentinelled by star
Of crystal even;
Around a harbor of the twilight glowing,
With jubilant waves about its gateways flowing

A city of the Land of Lost Delight,
On seas enchanted,
Presently to be lost in mist moon-white
And music-haunted;
Given but briefly to our raptured vision,
With all its opal towers and shrines elysian.

Had we some mystic boat with pearly oar
And wizard pilot,
To guide us safely by the siren shore
And cloudy islet,
We might embark and reach that shining portal
Beyond which linger dreams and joys immortal.

But we may only gaze with longing eyes
On those far, sparkling
Palaces in the fairy-peopled skies,
O'er waters darkling,
Until the winds of night come shoreward roaming,
And the dim west has only gray and gloaming.

Lucy Maud Montgomery

Sea-Fever

I must go down to the seas again, to the lonely sea
and the sky,
And all I ask is a tall ship and a star to steer her by,
And the wheel's kick and the wind's song and the
white sail's shaking,
And a grey mist on the sea's face and a grey dawn
breaking.

I must go down to the seas again, for the call of the
running tide
Is a wild call and a clear call that may not be
denied;
And all I ask is a windy day with the white clouds
flying,
And the flung spray and the blown spume, and the
sea-gulls crying.

I must go down to the seas again to the vagrant
gypsy life.
To the gull's way and the whale's way where the
wind's like a whetted knife;
And all I ask is a merry yarn from a laughing fellow-
rover,
And quiet sleep and a sweet dream when the long
trick's over.

John Masefield

Seal Lullaby

Oh! hush thee, my baby, the night is behind us,
    And black are the waters that sparkled so green.
The moon, o'er the combers, looks downward to
    find us
    At rest in the hollows that rustle between.
Where billow meets billow, there soft be thy pillow;
    Ah, weary wee flipperling, curl at thy ease!
The storm shall not wake thee, nor shark overtake
    thee,
    Asleep in the arms of the slow-swinging seas.

                                    Rudyard Kipling

St. Mary's Bells

It's pleasant in Holy Mary
By San Marie lagoon,
The bells they chime and jingle
From dawn to afternoon.

They rhyme and chime and mingle,
They pulse and boom and beat,
And the laughing bells are gentle
And the mournful bells are sweet.

Oh, who are the men that ring them,
The bells of San Marie,
Oh, who but sonsie seamen
Come in from over sea,

And merrily in the belfries
They rock and sway and hale,
And send the bells a-jangle,
And down the lusty ale.

It's pleasant in Holy Mary
To hear the beaten bells
Come booming into music,
Which throbs, and clangs, and swells,

From sunset till the daybreak.
From dawn to afternoon.

In port of Holy Mary
On San Marie Lagoon.

John Masefield

The Children of the Foam

OUT forever and forever,
Where our tresses glint and shiver
On the icy moonlit air;
Come we from a land of gloaming,
Children lost, forever homing,
Never, never reaching there;
Ride we, ride we, ever faster,
Driven by our demon master,
The wild wind in his despair.
Ride we, ride we, ever home,
Wan, white children of the foam.

In the wild October dawning,
When the heaven's angry awning
Leans to lakeward, bleak and drear;
And along the black, wet ledges,
Under icy, caverned edges,
Breaks the lake in maddened fear;
And the woods in shore are moaning;
Then you hear our weird intoning,
Mad, late children of the year;
Ride we, ride we, ever home,
Lost, white children of the foam.

All grey day, the black sky under,
Where the beaches moan and thunder,
Where the breakers spume and comb,
You may hear our riding, riding,
You may hear our voices chiding,
Under glimmer, under gloom;

Like a far-off infant wailing,
You may hear our hailing, hailing,
For the voices of our home;
Ride we, ride we, ever home,
Haunted children of the foam.

And at midnight, when the glimmer
Of the moon grows dank and dimmer,
Then we lift our gleaming eyes;
Then you see our white arms tossing,
Our wan breasts the moon embossing,
Under gloom of lake and skies;
You may hear our mournful chanting,
And our voices haunting, haunting,
Through the night's mad melodies;
Riding, riding, ever home,
Wild, white children of the foam.

There, forever and forever,
Will no demon-hate dissever
Peace and sleep and rest and dream:
There is neither fear nor fret there
When the tired children get there,
Only dews and pallid beam
Fall in gentle peace and sadness
Over long surcease of madness,
From hushed skies that gleam and gleam,
In the longed-for, sought-for home
Of the children of the foam.

There the streets are hushed and restful,
And of dreams is every breast full,

With the sleep that tired eyes wear;
There the city hath long quiet
From the madness and the riot,
From the failing hearts of care;
Balm of peacefulness ingliding,
Dream we through our riding, riding,
As we homeward, homeward fare;
Riding, riding, ever home,
Wild, white children of the foam.

Under pallid moonlight beaming,
Under stars of midnight gleaming,
And the ebon arch of night;
Round the rosy edge of morning,
You may hear our distant horning,
You may mark our phantom flight;
Riding, riding, ever faster,
Driven by our demon master,
Under darkness, under light;
Ride we, ride we, ever home,
Wild, white children of the foam.

William Wilfred Campbell

The City in the Sea

Lo! Death has reared himself a throne
In a strange city lying alone
Far down within the dim West,
Where the good and the bad and the worst and the
    best
Have gone to their eternal rest.
There shrines and palaces and towers
(Time-eaten towers that tremble not!)
Resemble nothing that is ours.
Around, by lifting winds forgot,
Resignedly beneath the sky
The melancholy waters lie.

No rays from the holy heaven come down
On the long night-time of that town;
But light from out the lurid sea
Streams up the turrets silently--
Gleams up the pinnacles far and free--
Up domes--up spires--up kingly halls--
Up fanes--up Babylon-like walls--
Up shadowy long-forgotten bowers
Of sculptured ivy and stone flowers--
Up many and many a marvellous shrine
Whose wreathed friezes intertwine
The viol, the violet, and the vine.
Resignedly beneath the sky
The melancholy waters lie.
So blend the turrets and shadows there
That all seem pendulous in air,
While from a proud tower in the town

Death looks gigantically down.

There open fanes and gaping graves
Yawn level with the luminous waves;
But not the riches there that lie
In each idol's diamond eye--
Not the gaily-jewelled dead
Tempt the waters from their bed;
For no ripples curl, alas!
Along that wilderness of glass--
No swellings tell that winds may be
Upon some far-off happier sea--
No heavings hint that winds have been
On seas less hideously serene.

But lo, a stir is in the air!
The wave--there is a movement there!
As if the towers had thrust aside,
In slightly sinking, the dull tide--
As if their tops had feebly given
A void within the filmy Heaven.
The waves have now a redder glow--
The hours are breathing faint and low--
And when, amid no earthly moans,
Down, down that town shall settle hence,
Hell, rising from a thousand thrones,
Shall do it reverence.

Edgar Allan Poe

The Convergence of the Twain
(Lines on the loss of the "Titanic")

I

    In a solitude of the sea
    Deep from human vanity,
And the Pride of Life that planned her, stilly couches she.

II

    Steel chambers, late the pyres
    Of her salamandrine fires,
Cold currents thrid, and turn to rhythmic tidal lyres.

III

    Over the mirrors meant
    To glass the opulent
The sea-worm crawls — grotesque, slimed, dumb, indifferent.

IV

    Jewels in joy designed
    To ravish the sensuous mind
Lie lightless, all their sparkles bleared and black and blind.

V

    Dim moon-eyed fishes near
    Gaze at the gilded gear
And query: "What does this vaingloriousness down here?" ...

VI

     Well: while was fashioning
     This creature of cleaving wing,
The Immanent Will that stirs and urges everything

VII

     Prepared a sinister mate
     For her — so gaily great —
A Shape of Ice, for the time far and dissociate.

VIII

     And as the smart ship grew
     In stature, grace, and hue,
In shadowy silent distance grew the Iceberg too.

IX

     Alien they seemed to be;
     No mortal eye could see
The intimate welding of their later history,

X

     Or sign that they were bent
     By paths coincident
On being anon twin halves of one august event,

XI

     Till the Spinner of the Years
     Said "Now!" And each one hears,
And consummation comes, and jars two
    hemispheres.

Thomas Hardy

The Coral Grove

Deep in the wave is a coral grove,
Where the purple mullet, and gold-fish rove,
Where the sea-flower spreads its leaves of
    blue,
That never are wet with falling dew,
But in bright and changeful beauty shine,
Far down in the green and glassy brine.
The floor is of sand, like the mountain drift,
And the pearl shells spangle the flinty snow;
From coral rocks the sea plants lift
Their boughs, where the tides and billows
    flow;
The water is calm and still below,
For the winds and waves are absent there,
And the sands are bright as the stars that
    glow
In the motionless fields of upper air . . .

James Gates Percival

52

The Fisherman

The water rushed, the water rose
A fisherman by the sea
Observed his line in deep repose,
Cool to his heart was he.
And while he sat and waited there,
He saw the waves divide,
And, lo! a maid, with glistening hair,
Sprang from the troubled tide.

She sang to him, she spoke to him:
"Why lure my kind away
With human wit and cunningly
To the deadly blaze of day?
If you could know how blithe and free
The fishes thrive below,
You would descend, with us to be,
And prosperous to grow."

"Do not the sun and moon take on
Refreshment in the sea?
Do not their faces billow-drawn
Loom twice as splendidly?
This sky-like depth, it calls you not--
This heaven of tranquil blue?
Your mirrored form enthralls you not
To seek the endless dew?"

The water rushed, the water rose
And wet his naked feet;
His heart with yearning swells and grows,

As when two lovers meet.
She spoke to him, she sang to him;
Then all with him was o'er,--
Half drew she him, half sank he in,--
He sank to rise no more.

Johann Wolfgang von Goethe
Translations of Edwin Zeydel and
Charles Brooks combined

The Flight of the Gulls

Out over the spaces,
The sunny, blue places,
    Of water and sky;
Where day on day merges
    In nights that reel by;
Through calms and through
    surges,
Through storming and lulls,
O, follow,
    Follow,
The flight of the gulls.

With wheeling and reeling,
With skimming and stealing,
    We wing with the wind,
Out over the heaving
Of grey waters, leaving
    The lands far behind,
And dipping ships' hulls.
O, follow,
    Follow,
The flight of the gulls.

Up over the thunder
Of reefs that lie under,
    And dead sailors' graves;
Like snowflakes in summer,
Like blossoms in winter,
    We float on the waves,

And the shore-tide that pulls.
O, follow,
  Follow,
The flight of the gulls.

Would you know the wild vastness
Of the lakes in their fastness,
  Their heaven's blue span;
Then come to this region,
  From the dwellings of man
Leave the life-care behind you,
That nature annuls,
And follow,
  Follow,
The flight of the gulls.

    William Wilfred Campbell

The Golden City of St. Mary

Out beyond the sunset, could I but find the way,
Is a sleepy blue laguna which widens to a bay,
And there's the Blessed City -- so the sailors say --
    The Golden City of St. Mary.

It's built of fair marble -- white -- without a stain,
And in the cool twilight when the sea-winds wane
The bells chime faintly, like a soft, warm rain,
    In the Golden City of St. Mary.

Among the green palm-trees where the fire-flies
    shine,
Are the white tavern tables where the gallants dine,
Singing slow Spanish songs like old mulled wine,
    In the Golden City of St. Mary.

Oh I'll be shipping sunset-wards and westward-ho
Through the green toppling combers a-shattering
    into snow,
Till I come to quiet moorings and a watch below,
    In the Golden City of St. Mary.

John Masefield

57

The Lanterns of St. Eulalie

In the October afternoon
Orange and purple and maroon,

Goes quiet Autumn, lamp in hand,
About the apple-colored land,

To light in every apple-tree
The Lanterns of St. Eulalie.

They glimmer in the orchard shade
Like fiery opals set in jade,—

Crimson and russet and raw gold,
Yellow and green and scarlet old.

And O when I am far away
By foaming reef or azure bay,

In crowded street or hot lagoon,
Or under the strange austral moon,—

When the homesickness comes to me
For the great marshes by the sea,

The running dikes, the brimming tide,
And the dark firs on Fundy side,

In dreams once more I shall behold,
Like signal lights, those globes of gold

Hung out in every apple-tree—
The Lanterns of St. Eulalie.

Bliss Carman

The Mermaidens

The little white mermaidens live in the sea,
In a palace of silver and gold;
And their neat little tails are all covered with
  scales,
Most beautiful for to behold.
On wild white horses they ride, they ride,
And in chairs of pink coral they sit;
They swim all the night, with a smile of
  delight,
And never feel tired a bit.

Laura E. Richards

The New Colossus

Not like the brazen giant of Greek fame,
With conquering limbs astride from land to land;
Here at our sea-washed, sunset gates shall stand
A mighty woman with a torch, whose flame
Is the imprisoned lightning, and her name
Mother of Exiles. From her beacon-hand
Glows world-wide welcome; her mild eyes
   command
The air-bridged harbor that twin cities frame.
"Keep, ancient lands, your storied pomp!" cries she
With silent lips. "Give me your tired, your poor,
Your huddled masses yearning to breathe free,
The wretched refuse of your teeming shore.
Send these, the homeless, tempest-tost to me,
I lift my lamp beside the golden door!"

Emma Lazarus

The Sea of Sunset

This is the land the sunset washes,
These are the banks of the Yellow Sea;
Where it rose, or whither it rushes,
These are the western mystery!

Night after night her purple traffic
Strews the landing with opal bales;
Merchantmen poise upon horizons,
Dip, and vanish with fairy sails.

Emily Dickinson

The Ship and her Makers

The Ore

Before Man's labouring wisdom gave me birth
I had not even seen the light of day;
Down in the central darkness of the earth,
Crushed by the weight of continents I lay,
Ground by the weight to heat, not knowing then
The Air, the light, the noise, the world of men.

The Trees

We grew on mountains where the glaciers cry,
Infinite sombre armies of us stood
Below the snow-peaks which defy the sky;
A song like the gods moaning filled our wood;
We knew no men our life was to stand staunch.
Singing our song, against the avalanche.

The Hemp and Flax

We were a million grasses on the hill,
A million herbs which bowed as the wind blew,
Trembling in every fibre, never still ;
Out of the summer earth sweet life we drew.
Little blue-flowered grasses up the glen,
Glad of the sun, what did we know of men?

The Workers

We tore the iron from the mountain's hold,
By blasting fires we smithied it to steel;
Out of the shapeless stone we learned to mould
The sweeping bow, the rectilinear keel;
We hewed the pine to plank, we split the fir,
We pulled the myriad flax to fashion her.

Out of a million lives our knowledge came,
A million subtle craftsmen forged the means;
Steam was our handmaid and our servant flame.
Water our strength, all bowed to our machines.
Out of the rock, the tree, the springing herb
We built this wandering beauty so superb.

The Sailors

We, who were born on earth and live by air,
Make this thing pass across the fatal floor,
The speechless sea; alone we commune there
Jesting with death, that ever open door.
Sun, moon and stars are signs by which we drive
This wind-blown iron like a thing alive.

The Ship

I march across great waters like a queen,
I whom so many wisdoms helped to make;
Over the uncruddled billows of seas green
I blanch the bubbled highway of my wake.
By me my wandering tenants clasp the hands,
And know the thoughts of men in other lands.

John Masefield

The Sound of the Sea

The sea awoke at midnight from its sleep,
And round the pebbly beaches far and wide
I heard the first wave of the rising tide
Rush onward with uninterrupted sweep;
A voice out of the silence of the deep,
A sound mysteriously multiplied
As of a cataract from the mountain's side,
Or roar of winds upon a wooded steep.
So comes to us at times, from the unknown
And inaccessible solitudes of being,
The rushing of the sea-tides of the soul;
And inspirations, that we deem our own,
Are some divine foreshadowing and foreseeing
Of things beyond our reason or control.

Henry Wadsworth Longfellow

The Sunken City

HARK! the faint bells of the sunken city
  Peal once more their wonted evening chime!
From the deep abysses floats a ditty,
  Wild and wondrous, of the olden time.

Temples, towers, and domes of many stories
  There lie buried in an ocean grave,—
Undescried, save when their golden glories
  Gleam, at sunset, through the lighted wave.

And the mariner who had seen them glisten,
  In whose ears those magic bells do sound,
Night by night bides there to watch and listen,
  Though death lurks behind each dark rock round.

So the bells of memory's wonder-city
  Peal for me their old melodious chime!
So my heart pours forth a changeful ditty,
  Sad and pleasant, from the bygone time.

Domes and towers and castles, fancy-builded,
  There lie lost to daylight's garish beams,—
There lie hidden till unveiled and gilded,
  Glory-gilded, by my nightly dreams!

And then hear I music sweet upknelling
  From many a well-known phantom band,
And, through tears, can see my natural dwelling
  Far off in the spirit's luminous land!

Wilhelm Mueller
Translated from the German by James
Clarence Mangan

The Voyagers

We shall launch our shallop on waters blue from
    some dim primrose shore,
We shall sail with the magic of dusk behind and
    enchanted coasts before,
Over oceans that stretch to the sunset land where
    lost Atlantis lies,
And our pilot shall be the vesper star that shines in
    the amber skies.

The sirens will call to us again, all sweet and
    demon-fair,
And a pale mermaiden will beckon us, with mist on
    her night-black hair;
We shall see the flash of her ivory arms, her
    mocking and luring face,
And her guiling laughter will echo through the great,
    wind-winnowed space.

But we shall not linger for woven spell, or sea-
    nymph's sorceries,
It is ours to seek for the fount of youth, and the gold
    of Hesperides,
Till the harp of the waves in its rhythmic beat keeps
    time to our pulses' swing,
And the orient welkin is smit to flame with auroral
    crimsoning.

And at last, on some white and wondrous dawn, we
    shall reach the fairy isle
Where our hope and our dream are waiting us, and

the to-morrows smile;
With song on our lips and faith in our hearts we sail
on our ancient quest,
And each man shall find, at the end of the voyage,
the thing he loves the best.

Lucy Maud Montgomery

The World Below the Brine

The world below the brine;
Forests at the bottom of the sea--the branches and
    leaves,
Sea-lettuce, vast lichens, strange flowers and
    seeds—
    the thick tangle, the openings, and the pink turf,
Different colors, pale gray and green, purple, white,
    and gold—the play of light through the water,
Dumb swimmers there among the rocks--coral,
    gluten, grass, rushes--
    and the aliment of the swimmers,
Sluggish existences grazing there, suspended, or
    slowly crawling close to the bottom,
The sperm-whale at the surface, blowing air and
    spray, or disporting with his flukes,
The leaden-eyed shark, the walrus, the turtle, the
    hairy sea-leopard, and the sting-ray;
Passions there--wars, pursuits, tribes--sight in
    those ocean-depths--
breathing that thick-breathing air, as so many do;
The change thence to the sight here, and to the
    subtle air breathed
by beings like us, who walk this sphere;
The change onward from ours, to that of beings
    who walk other spheres.

Walt Whitman

Trade Winds

In the harbour, in the island, in the Spanish Seas,
Are the tiny white houses and the orange trees,
And day-long, night-long, the cool and pleasant
     breeze
Of the steady Trade Winds blowing.

There is the red wine, the nutty Spanish ale,
The shuffle of the dancers, the old salt's tale,
The squeaking fiddle, and the soughing in the sail
Of the steady Trade Winds blowing.

And o' nights there's fire-flies and the yellow moon,
And in the ghostly palm-trees the sleepy tune
Of the quiet voice calling me, the long low croon
Of the steady Trade Winds blowing.

John Masefield

Wynken, Blynken, and Nod

Wynken, Blynken, and Nod one night
    Sailed off in a wooden shoe,—
Sailed on a river of crystal light
    Into a sea of dew.
"Where are you going, and what do you
    wish?"
    The old moon asked the three.
"We have come to fish for the herring-fish
    That live in this beautiful sea;
    Nets of silver and gold have we,"
        Said Wynken,
        Blynken,
        And Nod.

The old moon laughed and sang a song,
    As they rocked in the wooden shoe;
And the wind that sped them all night long
    Ruffled the waves of dew;
The little stars were the herring-fish
    That lived in the beautiful sea.
"Now cast your nets wherever you wish,—
    Never afraid are we!"
    So cried the stars to the fishermen three,
        Wynken,
        Blynken,
        And Nod.

All night long their nets they threw
    To the stars in the twinkling foam,—
Then down from the skies came the wooden

shoe,
Bringing the fishermen home:
'Twas all so pretty a sail, it seemed
As if it could not be;
And some folk thought 'twas a dream they'd
dreamed
Of sailing that beautiful sea;
But I shall name you the fishermen three:
Wynken,
Blynken,
And Nod.

Wynken and Blynken are two little eyes,
And Nod is a little head,
And the wooden shoe that sailed the skies
Is a wee one's trundle-bed;
So shut your eyes while Mother sings
Of wonderful sights that be,
And you shall see the beautiful things
As you rock in the misty sea
Where the old shoe rocked the fishermen
three:—
Wynken,
Blynken,
And Nod.

Eugene Field

II

Stories

The Fate of the Evangeline

Arthur Conan Doyle

First published in *Boy's Own Paper*, Christmas edition, December 1885. First book appearance-- *The Unknown Conan Doyle*, 1929

I

My wife and I often laugh when we happen to glance at some of the modern realistic sensational stories, for, however strange and exciting they may be we invariably come to the conclusion that they are tame compared to our own experiences when life was young with us.

More than once, indeed, she has asked me to write the circumstances down, but when I considered how few people there are in England who might remember the *Evangeline* or care to know the real history of her disappearance, it has seemed to me to be hardly worth while to revive the subject. Even here in Australia, however, we do occasionally see some reference to her in the papers or magazines, so that it is evident that there are those who have not quite forgotten the strange story: and so at this merry Christmastide I am tempted to set the matter straight.

At the time her fate excited a most intense and lively interest all over the British Islands, as was shown by the notices in the newspapers and by numerous letters which appeared upon the subject. As an example of this, as well as to give the facts in a succinct form, I shall preface this narrative by a few clippings chosen from many which we collected after the event, which are so numerous that my wife has filled a small scrapbook with them. This first one is from the "Inverness Gazette" of September 24th, 1873.

"PAINFUL OCCURRENCE IN THE HEBRIDES.— A sad accident, which it is feared has been attended with loss of life, has occurred at Ardvoe, which is a small uninhabited island lying about forty miles north-west of Harris and about half that distance south of the Flannons. It appears that a yacht named the Evangeline, belonging to Mr. Scholefield, jun., the son of the well-known banker of the firm Scholefield, Davies, and Co., had put in there, and that the passengers, with the two seamen who formed the crew, had pitched two tents upon the beach, in which they camped out for two or three days. This they did no doubt out of admiration for the rugged beauty of the spot, and perhaps from a sense of the novelty of their situation upon this lonely island. Besides Mr. Scholefield there were on the Evangeline a young lady named Miss Lucy Forrester, who is understood to be his fiancée, and her father, Colonel Forrester, of Teddington, near London. As the weather was very warm, the two gentlemen remained upon shore during the night, sleeping in one tent, while the seamen occupied the other. The young lady, however, was in the habit of rowing back to the yacht in the dinghy and sleeping in her own cabin, coming back by the same means in the morning.

One day, the third of their residence upon the island, Colonel Forrester, looking out of the tent at dawn, was astonished and horrified to see that the moorings of the boat had given way, and that she was drifting rapidly out to sea. He promptly gave the alarm, and Mr. Scholefield, with one of the sailors, attempted to swim out to her, but they found that the yacht, owing to the fresh breeze and the fact that one of the sails had been so clumsily furled as to offer a considerable surface to the wind, was making such headway that it was impossible to overtake her. When last seen she was drifting along in a west-sou'-westerly direction with the unfortunate young lady on board. To make matters worse, it was three days before the party on the island were able to communicate with a passing fishing-boat and inform them of the sad occurrence. Both before and since, the weather has been so tempestuous that there is little hope of the safety of the missing yacht. We hear, however, that a reward of a thousand pounds has been offered by the firm of Scholefield to the boat which finds her and of five thousand to the one which brings Miss Forrester back in safety. Apart from any recompense, however, we are sure that the chivalry of our brave fishermen will lead them to do everything in their power to succour this young lady, who is said to possess personal charms of the highest order. Our only grain of consolation is that the Evangeline was well provided both with provisions and with water."

This appeared upon September 24th, four days after the disappearance of the yacht. Upon the 25th the following telegram was sent from the north of Ireland:

"Portrush.—John Mullins, of this town, fisherman, reports that upon the morning of the 21st he sighted a yacht which answered to the description of the missing Evangeline. His own boat was at that time about fifty miles to the north of Malin Head, and was hove-to, the weather being very thick and dirty. The yacht passed within two hundred yards of his starboard quarter, but the fog was so great that he could not swear to her appearance. She was running in a westerly direction under a reefed mainsail and jib. *There was a man at the tiller.* He distinctly saw a woman on board, and thinks that she called out to him, but could not be sure owing to the howling of the wind."

I have many other extracts here expressive of the doubts and fears which existed as to the fate of the *Evangeline*, but I shall not quote one more than is necessary. Here is the Central News telegram which quashed the last lingering hopes of the most sanguine. It went the round of the papers upon the 3rd of October.

"Galway, October 2nd, 7.25 p.m.—The fishing boat Glenmullet has just come in, towing behind her a mass of wreckage, which leaves no doubt as to the fate of the unfortunate Evangeline and of the young lady who was on board of her. The fragments brought in consist of the bowsprit, figurehead, and part of the bows, with the name engraved upon it. From its appearance it is conjectured that the yacht was blown on to one of the dangerous reefs upon the north-west coast, and that after being broken up there this and possibly other fragments had drifted out to sea. Attached to it is a fragment of the fatal rope, the snapping of which was the original cause of the disaster. It is a stout cable of manilla hemp, and the fracture is a clean one—so clean as to suggest friction against a very sharp rock or the cut of a knife. Several boats have gone up and down the coast this evening in the hope of finding some more *débris* or of ascertaining with certainty the fate of the young lady."

From that day to this, however, nothing fresh has been learned of the fate of the *Evangeline* or of Miss Lucy Forrester, who was on board of her. These three extracts represent all that has ever been learned about either of them, and in these even there are several statements which the press at the time showed to be incredible. For example, how could the fisherman John Mullins say that he saw a man on board when Ardvoe is an unin- habited island, and therefore no one could possibly have got on board except Miss Forrester? It was clear that he was either mistaken in the boat or else that he imagined the man. Again, it was pointed out in a leader in the "Scotsman" that the conjecture that the rope was either cut by a rock or by a knife was manifestly absurd, since there are no rocks around Ardvoe, but a uniform sandy bottom, and it would be preposterous to suppose that Miss Forrester, who was a lady as remarkable for her firmness of mind as for her beauty, would deliberately sever the rope which attached her to her father, her lover, and to life itself. "It would be well," the "Scotsman" concluded, "if those who express opinions upon such subjects would bear in mind those simple rules as to the analysis of evidence laid down by Auguste Dupin. 'Exclude the impossible,' he remarks in one of Poe's immortal stories, 'and what is left, however improbable, must be the truth.' Now, since it is impossible that a rock divided the rope, and impossible that the young lady divided it, and doubly impossible that anybody else divided it, it follows that it parted of its own accord, either owing to some flaw in its texture or from some previous injury that it may have sustained. Thus this sad occurrence, about which conjecture is so rife, sinks at once into the category of common accidents, which, however deplorable, can neither be foreseen nor prevented."

There was one other theory which I shall just allude to before I commence my own personal narrative. That is the suggestion that either of the two sailors had had a spite against Mr. Scholefield or Colonel Forrester and had severed the rope out of revenge. That, however, is quite out of the question, for they were both men of good character and old servants of the Scholefields. My wife tells me that it is mere laziness which makes me sit with the scrapbook before me copying out all these old newspaper articles and conjectures. It is certainly the easiest way to tell my story, but I must now put them severely aside and tell you in my own words as concisely as I can what the real facts were.

* * * * *

My name is John Vincent Gibbs, and I am the son of Nathaniel Gibbs, formerly a captain in one of the West Indian regiments. My father was a very handsome man, and he succeeded in winning the heart of a Miss Leblanche, who was heiress to a good sugar plantation in Demerara. By this marriage my father became fairly rich, and, having left the army, he settled down to the life of a planter. I was born within a year of the marriage, but my mother never rose again from her bed, and my father was so broken-hearted at his loss that he pined away and followed her to the grave within a few months.

I have thus never known either of my two parents, and the loss of their control, combined perhaps with my tropical birthplace, made me, I fear, somewhat headstrong and impetuous.

Immediately that I became old enough to be my own master I sold the estate and invested the money in Government stock in such a way as to insure me an income of fifteen hundred a year for life. I then came to Europe, and for a long time led a strange Bohemian life, flitting from one University to another, and studying spasmodically those sub-jects which interested me. I went to Heidelberg for a year in order to read chemistry and metaphysics, and when I returned to London I plunged for the first time into society. I was then twenty-four years of age, dark-haired, dark-eyed, swarthy, with a smattering of all knowledge and a mastery of none.

It was during this season in London that I first saw Lucy Forrester. How can I describe her so as to give even the faintest conception of her beauty? To my eyes no woman ever had been or could be so fair. Her face, her voice, her figure, every movement and action, were part of one rare and harmonious whole. Suffice it that I loved her the very evening that I saw her, and that I went on day after day increasing and nourishing this love until it possessed my whole being.

At first my suit prospered well. I made the acquaintance of her father, an elderly soldier, and became a frequent visitor at the house. I soon saw that the keynote of Miss Forrester's character was her intense devotion to her father, and accordingly I strove to win her regard by showing extreme deference and attention to him. I succeeded in interesting her in many topics, too, and we became very friendly. At last I ventured to speak to her of love, and told her of the passion which consumed me. I suppose I spoke wildly and fiercely, for she was frightened and shrank from me.

I renewed the subject another day, however, with better success. She confessed to me then that she loved me, but added firmly that she was her father's only child, and that it was her duty to devote her life to comforting his declining years. Her personal feelings, she said, should never prevent her from performing that duty. It mattered not. The confession that I was dear to her filled me with ecstasy. For the rest I was content to wait.

During this time the colonel had favoured my suit. I have no doubt that some gossip had exaggerated my wealth and given him false ideas of my importance. One day in conversation I told him what my resources were. I saw his face change as he listened to me, and from that moment his demeanour altered.

It chanced that about the same time young Scholefield, the son of the rich banker, came back from Oxford, and having met Lucy, became very marked in his attentions to her. Colonel Forrester at once encouraged his addresses in every possible way, and I received a curt note from him informing me that I should do well to discontinue my visits.

I still had hopes that Lucy would not be influenced by her father's mercenary schemes. For days I frequented her usual haunts, seeking an opportunity of speaking to her. At last I met her alone one morning in St. James's Park. She looked me straight in the face, and there was an expression of great tenderness and sadness in her eyes, but she would have passed me without speaking. All the blood seemed to rush into my head, and I caught her by the wrist to detain her.

"You have given me up, then?" I cried. "There is no longer any hope for me."

"Hush, Jack!" she said, for I had raised my voice excitedly. "I warned you how it would be. It is my father's wish and I must obey him, whatever it costs. Let me go now. You must not hold me any more."

"And there is no hope?"

"You will soon forget me," she said. "You must not think of me again."

"Ah, you are as bad as he," I cried, excitedly. "I read it in your eyes. It is the money—the wretched money." I was sorry for the words the moment after I had said them, but she had passed gravely on, and I was alone.

I sat down upon one of the benches in the park, and rested my head upon my hands. I felt numbed and stupefied. The world and everything in it had changed for me during the last ten minutes. People passed me as I sat—people who laughed and joked and gossiped. It seemed to me that I watched them almost as a dead man might watch the living. I had no sympathy with their little aims, their little pleasures and their little pains. "I'll get away from the whole drove of them," I said, as I rose from my seat. "The women are false and the men are fools, and everything is mean and sordid." My first love had unhappily converted me to cynicism, rash and foolish as I was, as it has many such a man before.

For many months I travelled, endeavouring by fresh scenes and new experiences to drive away the memory of that fair false face. At Venice I heard that she was engaged to be married to young Scholefield. "He's got a lot of money," this tourist said—it was at the table d'hôte at the Hotel de l'Europe. "It's a splendid match for her." For *her*!

When I came back to England I flitted restlessly about from one place to another, avoiding the haunts of my old associates, and leading a lonely and gloomy life. It was about this time that the idea first occurred to me of separating my person from mankind as widely as my thoughts and feelings were distinct from theirs. My temperament was, I think, naturally a somewhat morbid one, and my disappointment had made me a complete misanthrope. To me, without parents, friends, or relations, Lucy had been everything, and now that she was gone the very sight of a human face was hateful to me. Loneliness in a wilderness, I reflected, was less irksome than loneliness in a city. In some wild spot I might be face to face with nature and pursue the studies into which I had plunged once more, without interruption or disturbance.

As this resolution began to grow upon me I thought of this island of Ardvoe, which, curiously enough, had been first mentioned to me by Scholefield on one of the few occasions when we had been together in the house of the Forresters. I had heard him speak of its lonely and desolate position, and of its beauty, for his father had estates in Skye, from which he was wont to make yachting trips in summer, and in one of these he had visited the island. It frequently happened, he said, that no one set foot upon it during the whole year, for there was no grass for sheep, and nothing to attract fisher-men. This, I thought, would be the very place for me.

Full of my new idea, I travelled to Skye, and from thence to Uist. There I hired a fishing-boat from a man named McDiarmid, and sailed with him and his son to the island. It was just such a place as I had imagined—rugged and desolate, with high, dark crags rising up from a girdle of sand. It had been once, McDiarmid said, a famous emporium for the goods of smugglers, which used to be stored there, and then conveyed over to the Scotch coast as occasion served. He showed me several of the caves of these gentry, and one in particular, which I immediately determined should be my own future dwelling. It was approached by a labyrinth of rocky paths, which effectually secured it against any intruder, while it was roomy inside, and lit up by an aperture in the rock above, which might be covered over in wet weather.

The fisherman told me that his father had pointed the spot out to him, but that it was not commonly known to the rare visitors who came to the island. There was abundance of fresh water, and fish were to be caught in any quantity.

I was so well satisfied with my survey that I returned to Scotland with the full intention of realising my wild misanthropical scheme.

In Glasgow I purchased most of the more important things that I wanted to take with me. These included a sleeping bag, such as is used in the Arctic seas; several mathematical and astronomical instruments; a very varied and extensive assortment of books, including nearly every modern work upon chemistry and physics; a double-barrelled fowling-piece, fishing-tackle, lamps, candles, and oil. Subsequently at Oban and Stornoway I purchased two bags of potatoes, a sack of flour, and a quantity of tinned meats, together with a small stove. All these things I conveyed over in McDiarmid's boat, having already bound both himself and his son to secrecy upon the matter—a promise which, as far as I know, neither of them ever broke. I also had a table and chair conveyed across, with a plentiful supply of pens, ink, and paper.

All these things were stowed away in the cave, and I then requested McDiarmid to call upon the first of each month, or as soon after as the weather permitted, in case I needed anything. This he promised to do, and having been well paid for his services, he departed, leaving me upon the island.

It was a strange sensation to me when I saw the brown sail of his boat sinking below the horizon, until at last it disappeared, and left one broad, unbroken sheet of water before me. That boat was the last tie which bound me to the human race. When it had vanished, and I returned into my cave with the knowledge that no sight or sound could jar upon me now, I felt the first approach to satisfaction which I had had through all those weary months. A fire was sparkling in the stove, for fuel was plentiful on the island, and the long stove-pipe had been so arranged that it projected through the aperture above, and so carried the smoke away. I boiled some potatoes and made a hearty meal, after which I wrote and read until nightfall, when I crept into my bag and slept soundly.

It might weary my readers should I speak of my existence upon this island, though the petty details of my housekeeping seem to interest my dear wife more than anything else, and ten years have not quite exhausted her questions upon the subject. I cannot say that I was happy, but I was less unhappy than I could have believed it possible. At times, it is true, I was plunged into the deepest melancholy, and would remain so for days, without energy enough to light my fire or to cook my food. On these occasions I would wander aimlessly among the hills and along the shore until I was worn out with fatigue. After these attacks, however, I would become, if not placid, at least torpid for a time. Occasionally I could even smile at my strange life as an anchorite, and speculate as to whether the lord of the manor, since I presumed the island belonged to some one, would become aware of my existence, and if so, whether he would evict me ignominiously, or claim a rent for my little cavern.

II

Three months had passed, as I knew by the regular visits of the worthy fisherman, when the event occurred which altered the course of my whole life, and led in the end to the writing of this narrative.

I had been out all day surveying my little kingdom, and having returned about four o'clock, had settled down to Ricardo's "Principles of Political Economy," of which work I was writing a critical analysis. I had been writing about three hours, and the waning light (it was in September) was warning me that the time had come to stop, when suddenly, to my intense astonishment, I heard a human voice. Crusoe, when he saw the footstep, could hardly have been more surprised. My first idea was that some unforeseen circumstance had induced McDiarmid to come across before his time, and that he was hailing me; but a moment's reflection showed me that the voice which I had heard was very different from the rough Gaelic accents of the fisherman. As I sat pen in hand, wondering and listening, a peal of laughter rose up from the beach. An unreasoning indignation at this intrusion on my privacy then took possession of me, and I rushed out of my cave and peered over the rocks to see who the invaders might be.

Down beneath me in the bay a trim little yacht of five-and-twenty tons or thereabouts was riding at anchor. On the beach two yachtsmen—a young man and an old—were endeavouring with the aid of a sailor to raise a canvas tent, and were busily engaged knocking pegs into the crumbling sand and fastening ropes to them. Between the shore and the yacht there was a small boat rowed by one man, and in the sheets there sat a lady. When the boat reached the shore one of the yachtsmen, the younger of the two, ran down and handed its passenger out. The instant she stood erect I recognised her. Even after the lapse of ten years I feel again the rush and whirlwind of emotion which came over me when I saw once more in this strange place the woman whom I loved better than all the world besides.

At first it seemed so extraordinary, so utterly inexplicable, that I could only surmise that she and her father and lover (for I had now recognised the two men also) had heard of my presence here and had come with the intention of insulting me. This was the mad notion which came into my disordered brain. The unconcerned air of the party showed, however, that this could not be. On second thoughts I convinced myself that it was no very wonderful coincidence after all. No doubt Schole-field was taking up the young lady and her father to pay a visit to his rich friends in Skye. If so, what more natural than that in passing they should visit this island concerning which I remembered that Lucy had expressed interest and curiosity when Scholefield spoke of it originally? It seemed to me now to be such a natural sequence of events that my only wonder was that the possibility of it had not occurred to me earlier.

The tent was soon up, and they had supper inside it, after raising another smaller tent for the two seamen. It was evident that the whole party intended to camp out for a time.

I crept down towards the beach after it was dark, and came as near to them as I dared. After a time Scholefield sang a sea song; and then, after some persuasion, she sang too—a melancholy ballad, one which had been a favourite of mine in the old days in London. What would she have thought, I wondered, could she have seen me, unshaven and dishevelled, crouching like a wild beast among the rocks! My heart was full, and I could bear it no longer. I went back to my lonely cave with all my old wounds ripped open afresh.

About ten o'clock I saw her in the moonlight go down to the beach alone, and row to the yacht, where she fastened the dinghy astern. She was always proud, I remembered, of being at home upon the water. I knew then for certain that she was not married yet, and a gush of senseless joy and hope rose up in my bosom.

I saw her row back in the morning, and the party breakfasted together in the tent. Afterwards they spent the day in exploring the island and in gathering the rare shells which are to be found upon the beach. They never came my way—indeed the rocks among which my cave lay were well-nigh inaccessible to any one who did not know the steep and intricate pathway. I watched the lady wandering along the sands, and once she passed immediately beneath my citadel. Her face was pale, I thought, and she seemed graver than when I saw her last, but otherwise there was no change. Her blue yachting costume with white lace and gilt buttons suited her to perfection. Strange how small details may stick in the memory!

It was on the evening of the second day of their visit that I found that the stock of fresh water which I usually kept in my cave had run short, which necessitated my going to the stream for more. It was about a hundred yards off, and not far from the tent, but it seemed to me that since darkness had set in I should be running no risk of discovery; so taking my bucket in my hand I set off. I had filled it and was about to return when I heard the footsteps and voices of two men close to me, and had hardly time to crouch down behind a furze bush when they stopped almost within arm's length of me.

"Help you!" I heard one of them say, whom I at once identified as old Forrester. "My dear fellow, you must help yourself. You must be patient and you must be resolute. When I broached the matter to her she said that she had obeyed me in not speaking to the other, but when I asked for more than that I exceeded the claims which a father has upon a daughter. Those were her very words."

"I can't make it out," the other said peevishly; "you always hold out hopes, but they never come to anything. She is kind to me and friendly, but no more. The fellows at the club think that I am engaged to her. Everybody thinks so."

"So you will be, my boy, so you will be," Forrester answered. "Give her time."

"It's that black chap Gibbs who runs in her head," said Scholefield. "The fellow is dead, I believe, or gone mad, as I always said he would. Anyway he has disappeared from the world, but that seems to make no difference to her."

"Pshaw!" the other answered. "Out of sight is out of mind, sooner or later. You will have exceptional opportunities at Skye, so make the most of them. For my part I promise to put on all the pressure I can. At present we must go down to the tent or she'll think we are lost," with which they moved off, and their steps died away in the distance.

I stood up after they were gone like one in a dream, and slowly carried back my bucket. Then I sat down upon my chair and leaned my head upon my hands, while my mind was torn by conflicting emotions. She was true to me then. She had never been engaged to my rival. Yet there was the old prohibition of her parent, which had no doubt the same sacred weight with her as ever. I was really no nearer her than before. But how about this conspiracy which I had overheard—this plot between a mercenary father and a mean-spirited suitor. Should I, ought I, to allow her to be bullied by the one or cajoled by the other into forsaking me? Never! I would appeal to her. I would give her one more chance at least of judging between her father and myself. Surely, I thought, I who love her so tenderly have more claim upon her than this man who would sell her to the highest bidder.

Then in a moment it came into my head how I could take her away from them, so that no one should stand between us, and I might plead my cause without interruption. It was such a plan as could only have occurred perhaps to a man of my impetuous nature. I knew that if once she left the island I might never have the chance again. There was but one way to do it, and I was determined that it should be done.

All night long I paced about my cave pondering over the details of my scheme. I would have put it into execution at once, but the sky was covered with clouds and the night was exceptionally dark. Never did time pass more slowly. At last the first cold grey light began to show upon the horizon and to spread slowly along it. I thrust a clasp knife into my pocket and as much money as I had in the cave. Then I crept down to the beach, some distance from the sleeping party, and swam out to the yacht. The ladder by which Lucy had got on board the night before was still hanging down, and by it I climbed on board. Moving softly so as not to awake her, I shook out enough of one of the sails to catch the breeze, and then stooping over the bows

I cut the thick rope by which we were moored. For a minute or so the yacht drifted aimlessly, and then getting some way on her she answered the helm, and stood out slowly towards the Atlantic.

Do not misunderstand me. I had no intention of forcing the lady's inclinations in any way, or compelling her to break her promise to her father. I was not base enough for that. My sole and only object was to have an opportunity of appealing to her, and pleading my cause for the last time. If I had not known, on the authority of her suitor, that she still loved me, I would have cut my right hand off as soon as cut that cable. As it was, if I could persuade her to be my wife we could run down to Ireland or back to Oban, and be married by special licence before the prisoners at Ardvoe could get away. If, on the other hand, she refused to have anything to do with me, I would loyally take the *Evangeline* back to her moorings and face the consequences, whatever they might be. Some have blamed me for putting the lady in such a compromising situation. Before they judge they must put themselves in my position, with but one chance of making life happy, and that chance depending upon prompt action. My savage life, too, may have somewhat blunted my regard for the conventionalities of civilisation.

As the boat slowly headed out to sea I heard a great outcry upon the beach, and saw Forrester and Scholefield, with the two sailors, running frantically about. I kept myself carefully out of sight.

Presently Scholefield and one of the sailors dashed into the water, but after swimming a little way they gave it up as hopeless, for the breeze was very fresh, and even with our little rag of canvas we could not have been going less than five knots. All this time Miss Forrester had not been disturbed, nor was there anything to let her know that the yacht was under way, for the tossing was no greater than when she was at anchor.

III

The moorings had been at the south end of the island, and as the wind was cast, we headed straight out to the Atlantic. I did not put up any more sail yet, for it would be seen by those we had left, and I wished at present to leave them under the impression that the yacht had drifted away by accident, so that if they found any means of communicating with the mainland they might start upon a wrong scent. After three hours, however, the island being by that time upon the extreme horizon, I hoisted the mainsail and jib.

I was busily engaged in tugging at the halliards, when Miss Forrester, fully dressed, stepped out of her cabin and came upon deck. I shall never forget the expression of utter astonishment which came over her beautiful features when she realised that she was out at sea and with a strange companion. She gazed at me with, at first, terror as well as surprise. No doubt, with my long dark hair and beard, and tattered clothing, I was not a very reassuring object.

The instant I opened my lips to address her, however, she recognised me, and seemed to comprehend the situation.

"Mr. Gibbs," she cried. "Jack, what have you done? You have carried me away from Ardvoe. Oh, take me back again! What will my poor father do?"

"He's all right," I said. "He is hardly so very thoughtful about you, and may not mind doing without you now for a little." She was silent for a while, and leaned against the companion rail, endeavouring to collect herself.

"I can hardly realise it," she said, at last. "How could you have come here, and why are we at sea? What is your object, Jack? What are you about to do?"

"My only object is this," I said, tremblingly, coming up closer to her. "I wished to be able to have a chance of talking to you alone without interruption. The whole happiness of my life depends upon it. That is why I have carried you off like this. All I ask you to do is to answer one or two questions, and I will promise to do your bidding. Will you do so?"

"Yes," she said, "I will."

She kept her eyes cast down and seemed to avoid my gaze. "Do you love this man Scholefield?" I asked.

"No," she answered, with decision.

"Will you ever marry him?"

"No," she answered again.

"Now, Lucy," I said, "speak the truth fearlessly, let me entreat you, for the happiness of both of us depends upon it. Do you still love me?"

She never spoke, but she raised her head and I read her answer in her eyes. My heart overflowed with joy.

"Then, my darling," I cried, taking her hand, "if you love me and I love you, who is to come between us? Who dare part us?"

She was silent, but did not attempt to escape from my arm.

"Not your father," I said. "He has no power or right over you. You know well that if one who was richer than Scholefield appeared to-morrow he would bid you smile upon him without a thought as to your own feelings. You can in such circumstances owe him no allegiance as to giving yourself for mere mercenary reasons to those you in heart abhor."

"You are right, Jack. I do not," she answered, speaking very gently, but very firmly. "I am sorry that I left you as I did in St. James's Park. Many a time since I have bitterly regretted it. Still at all costs I should have been true to my father if he had been true to me. But he has not been so. Though he knows my dislike to Mr. Scholefield he has continually thrown us together as on this yachting excursion, which was hateful to me from the first. Jack," she continued, turning to me, "you have been true to me through everything. If you still love me I am yours from this moment—yours entirely and for ever. I will place myself in their power no more."

Then in that happy moment I was repaid for all the long months of weariness and pain. We sat for hours talking of our thoughts and feelings since our last sad parting, while the boat drifted aimlessly among the tossing waves, and the sails flapped against the spars above our heads. Then I told her how I had swum off and cut the cable of the *Evangeline*.

"But, Jack," she said, "you are a pirate; you will be prosecuted for carrying off the boat."

"They may do what they like now," I said, defiantly; "I have gained you, in carrying off the boat."

"But what will you do now?" she asked.

"I will make for the north of Ireland," I said; "then I shall put you under the protection of some good woman until we can get a special licence and be able to defy your father. I shall send the *Evangeline* back to Ardvoe or to Skye. We are going to have some wind, I fear. You will not be afraid, dear?"

"Not while I am with you," she answered, calmly.

The prospect was certainly not a reassuring one. The whole eastern horizon was lined by great dark clouds, piled high upon each other, with that lurid tinge about them which betokens violent wind. Already the first warning blasts came whistling down upon us, heeling our little craft over till her gunwale lay level with the water. It was impossible to beat back to the Scotch coast, and our best chance of safety lay in running before the gale. I took in the topsail and flying-jib, and reefed down the mainsail; then I lashed everything moveable in case of our shipping a sea. I wished Lucy to go below to her cabin, but she would not leave me, and remained by my side.

As the day wore on the occasional blasts increased into a gale, and the gale into a tempest. The night set in dark and dreary, and still we sped into the Atlantic. The *Evangeline* rose to the seas like a cork, and we took little or no water aboard. Once or twice the moon peeped out for a few moments between the great drifting cloud-banks. Those brief intervals of light showed us the great wilderness of black, tossing waters which stretched to the horizon. I managed to bring some food and water from the cabin while Lucy held the tiller, and we shared it together. No persuasions of mine could induce her to leave my side for a moment.

With the break of day the wind appeared to gain more force than ever, and the great waves were so lofty that many of them rose high above our masthead. We staggered along under our reefed sail, now rising upon a billow, from which we looked down on two great valleys before and behind us, then sinking down into the trough of the sea until it seemed as if we could never climb the green wall beyond. By dead reckoning I calculated that we had been blown clear of the north coast of Ireland. It would have been madness to run towards an unknown and dangerous shore in such weather, but I steered a course now two more points to the south, so as not to get blown too far from the west coast in case that we had passed Malin Head. During the morning Lucy thought that she saw the loom of a fishing-boat, but neither of us were certain, for the weather had become very thick. This must have been the boat of the man Mullins, who seems to have had a better view of us than we had of him.

All day (our second at sea) we continued to steer in a south-westerly direction. The fog had increased and become so thick that from the stern we could hardly see the end of the bowsprit. The little vessel had proved herself a splendid sea boat, and we had both become so reconciled to our position, and so confident in her powers, that neither of us thought any longer of the danger of our position, especially as the wind and sea were both abating. We were just congratulating each other upon this cheering fact, when an unexpected and terrible catastrophe overtook us.

It must have been about seven in the evening, and I had gone down to rummage in the lockers and find something to eat, when I heard Lucy give a startled cry above me. I sprang upon deck instantly. She was standing up by the tiller peering out into the mist.

"Jack," she cried. "I hear voices. There is some one close to us."

"Voices!" I said; "impossible. If we were near land we should hear the breakers."

"Hist!" she cried, holding up her hand. "Listen!"

We were standing together straining our ears to catch every sound, when suddenly and swiftly there emerged from the fog upon our starboard bow a long line of Roman numerals with the figure of a gigantic woman hovering above them. There was no time for thought or preparation. A dark loom towered above us, taking the wind from our sails, and then a great vessel sprang upon us out of the mist as a wild beast might upon its prey. Instinctively, as I saw the monster surging down upon us, I flung one of the life-belts, which was hanging round the tiller, over Lucy's head, and seizing her by the waist, I sprang with her into the sea.

What happened after that it is hard to tell. In such moments all idea of time is lost. It might have been minutes or it might have been hours during which I swam by Lucy's side, encouraging her in every possible way to place full confidence in her belt and to float without struggling. She obeyed me to the letter, like a brave girl as she was. Every time I rose to the top of a wave I looked around for some sign of our destroyer, but in vain. We joined our voices in a cry for aid, but no answer came back except the howling of the wind. I was a strong swimmer, but hampered with my clothes my strength began gradually to fail me. I was still by Lucy's side, and she noticed that I became feebler.

"Trust to the belt, my darling, whatever happens," I said.

She turned her tender face towards me.

"If you leave me I shall slip it off," she answered.

Again I came to the top of a great roller, and looked round. There was nothing to be seen. But hark! what was that? A dull clanking noise came on my ears, which was distinct from the splash of the sea. It was the sound of oars in rowlocks. We gave a last feeble cry for aid. It was answered by a friendly shout, and the next that either of us remember was when we came to our senses once more and found ourselves in warm and comfortable berths with kind anxious faces around us. We had both fainted while being lifted into the boat.

The vessel was a large Norwegian sailing barque, the *Freyja*, of five hundred tons, which had started five days before from Bergen, and was bound for Adelaide in Australia. Nothing could exceed the kindness of Captain Thorbjorn and his crew to the two unfortunates whom they had picked out of the Atlantic Ocean. The watch on deck had seen us, but too late to prevent a collision. They had at once dropped a boat, which was about to return to the ship in despair, when that last cry reached their ears.

Captain Thorbjorn's wife was on board, and she at once took my dear companion under her care. We had a pleasant and rapid voyage to Adelaide, where we were duly married in the presence of Madame Thorbjorn and of all the officers of the *Freyja*.

After our marriage I went upcountry, and having taken a large farm there, I remained a happy and prosperous man. A sum of money was duly paid over to the firm of Scholefield, coming they knew not whence, which represented the value of the *Evangeline*.

One of the first English mails which followed us to Australia announced the death of Colonel Forrester, who fractured his skull by falling down the marble steps of a Glasgow hotel. Lucy was terribly grieved, but new associations and daily duties gradually overcame her sorrow.

Since then neither of us have anything to bind us to the old country, nor do we propose to return to it. We read the English periodicals, however, and have amused ourselves from time to time in noticing the stray allusions to the yacht *Evangeline*, and the sad fate of the young lady on board her. This short narrative of the real facts may therefore prove interesting to some few who have not forgotten what is now an old story, and some perhaps to whom the circumstances are new may care to hear a strange chapter in real life.

Taman

Written in 1839 by Mikhail Lermontov—
A story which also serves as a chapter in his novel,
A Hero of Our Time.

This is a combination of several English translations.

The story is told through the eyes of "Pechorin," a
character created by the author through his observations
of real people and events. Pechorin is a young Russian
officer serving in the Caucasus.

Taman is the nastiest of all the coastal villages of
Russia. It was there that I narrowly escaped death,
first by starvation and then by drowning.

I arrived late at night by carriage. The driver
stopped the tired horses at the gate of Taman's
only stone-built house, which stood at the entrance
to the town. The sentry, a Cossack from the Black
Sea, hearing the jingle of our harness bells, cried
out, sleepily, in his barbarous voice, "Who goes
there?"

A Cossack sergeant and a corporal came out. I
explained that I was an officer under orders to
report for duty, and I demanded official quarters.

The corporal conducted us around town in search
of lodging, but all the huts we drove up to were

occupied. The weather was cold; I had not slept for three nights; I was tired and began to lose my temper.

"Take me somewhere or other, you wretch!" I cried. "Even to the devil himself, so long as he has room to put me up!"

"There is one other lodging," answered the corporal, scratching his head. "Only you won't like it, sir. It is eerie!"

Failing to grasp the exact significance of the last phrase, I ordered him to go on. After a lengthy trip over small muddy roads, at the sides of which I could see nothing but old fences, we drove up to a small cabin, situated right next to the sea.

The full moon was shining on the little reed-thatched roof and the white walls of my new dwelling. In the courtyard, which was surrounded by a wall of cobblestone, there stood another miserable hovel, smaller and older than the first and all askew.

The shore descended precipitously to the sea, almost from the cabin's very walls, and down below, with incessant murmur, splashed the dark blue waves. The moon gazed softly upon the waters, restless but obedient to it, and I was able by its light to distinguish two ships lying at some distance from the shore, their black rigging motionless and standing out, like cobwebs, against the pale line of the horizon.

"There are vessels in the harbor," I said to myself. "Tomorrow I will set out for Gelenjik."

I had with me, in the capacity of a soldier-servant, a Cossack of the frontier army. Ordering him to take down the luggage and dismiss the driver, I began to call the master of the house. No answer! I knocked. All was silent within. What could it mean? At length a boy of about fourteen crept out from the hall.

"Where is the master?"

"There isn't one."

"What! No master?"

"None!"

"And the mistress?"

"She has gone off to the village."

"Who will open the door for me, then?" I said, giving it a kick and unintentionally opening it.

A breath of moisture-laden air was wafted from the hut. I struck a match and held it to the boy's face. It lit up two white eyes. He was totally blind, obviously so from birth. He stood stock-still before me, and I began to examine his features.

I confess that I have a violent prejudice against all blind, one-eyed, deaf, dumb, legless, arm-less, hunchbacked, and other such people. I have observed that there is always a certain strange connection between a man's exterior and his soul; as if when the body loses a limb, the soul also loses some power of feeling.

And so I began to examine the blind boy's face. But what could be read upon a face from which the eyes were missing? . . . For a long time I gazed at him with involuntary compassion, when suddenly a scarcely perceptible smile flitted over his thin lips. This produced, I know not why, a most unpleasant impression upon me. I began to feel a suspicion that the blind boy was not so blind as he appeared to be. In vain I endeavored to convince myself that it was impossible to fake blindness; and besides, what reason could there be for doing such a thing? But I could not dispel my suspicions. I am easily swayed by prejudice.

"You are the master's son?" I asked at length.

"No."

"Who are you, then?"

"An orphan — a poor boy."

"Has the mistress any children?"

"No, her daughter ran away across the sea with a Tartar."

"What sort of a Tartar?"

"The devil only knows! A Crimean Tartar, a boatman from Kerch."

I entered the hut. Its whole furniture consisted of two benches and a table, together with an enormous chest near the stove. There was not a single religious icon to be seen on the wall — a bad sign! The sea-wind burst in through the broken window pane.

I drew a wax candle end from my suitcase, lit it, and began to unpack my things. My sabre and gun I placed in a corner; my pistols I laid on the table. I spread my felt cloak out on one bench, and my Cossack put his on the other.

In ten minutes he was snoring, but I could not fall asleep — the image of the boy with the white eyes kept hovering before me in the dark.

About an hour passed thus. The moon shone in at the window and its rays played along the earthen floor of the hut. Suddenly a shadow flitted across the bright strip of moonshine reflected on the floor. I raised myself up a little and glanced out of the

window. Again somebody ran by and disappeared
— heaven knows where! It seemed impossible for
anyone to descend the steep cliff overhanging the
shore, but that was the only thing that could have
happened.

I rose, threw on my tunic, girded on a dagger, and
with the utmost quietness went out of the hut. The
blind boy was coming towards me. I hid by the
fence, and he passed by me with a sure but
cautious step. He was carrying a parcel under his
arm. He turned towards the harbor and began to
descend a steep and narrow path.

"On that day the dumb will cry out and the blind will
see," I said to myself, following him just closely
enough to keep him in sight.

Meanwhile the moon was becoming overcast by
clouds, and a mist had risen upon the sea. The
lantern at the stern of the closer ship was scarcely
visible through the mist. Along the shore, there
glimmered the foam of the waves, which by rolling
every moment threatened to submerge the fragile
light.

Descending with difficulty, I stole along the steep
cliff. All at once I saw the blind boy come to a
standstill and then turn sharply to the right. He
walked so close to the water's edge that it seemed
as if the waves might at any moment seize him and
carry him off. But, judging by the confidence with

114

which he stepped from rock to rock and avoided the water channels, this was evidently not the first time that he had made this journey. Finally he stopped, as though listening for something, squatted down upon the ground, and laid the parcel beside him. Concealing myself behind a projecting rock on the shore, I kept watch on his movements. After a few minutes, a white figure made its appearance from the opposite direction. It came up to the blind boy and sat down beside him. At times the wind wafted their conversation to me.

"Well?" said a woman's voice. "The storm is violent; Yanko will not be here."

"Yanko is not afraid of the storm!" the other replied.

"The mist is thickening," rejoined the woman's voice, sadness in its tone.

"In the mist it is all the easier to slip past the patrol boats," was the answer.

"And if he is drowned?"

"Well, what then? On Sunday you won't have a new ribbon to wear at church." An interval of silence followed. One thing, however, struck me — in talking to me the blind boy spoke in the Ukrainian dialect, but now he was expressing himself in pure Russian.

"You see, I am right!" the blind boy went on, clapping his hands. "Yanko is not afraid of sea, nor winds, nor mist, nor coast guards! Just listen! That is not the water splashing. You can't deceive me — it is his long oars."

The woman sprang up and began anxiously to gaze into the distance.

"You are wrong!" she said. "I cannot see anything."

I confess that, much as I tried to make out in the distance something resembling a boat, my efforts were unsuccessful.

About ten minutes passed like this, when a black speck appeared among the mountainous waves! At one moment it grew larger; at another, smaller. Slowly rising upon the crests of the waves and swiftly descending from them, the boat drew near to the shore. "He must be a brave sailor," I thought, "to have determined to cross fourteen miles of strait on a night like this, and he must have had strong reasons for doing so."

Reflecting thus, I gazed with an uncontrollable throbbing of my heart at the poor boat. It dived like a duck, and then, with rapidly swinging oars — like wings — it sprang forth from the abyss amid the raging foam. "Ah!" I thought, "it will be dashed against the shore with all its force and broken to pieces!" But it turned aside adroitly and leaped unharmed into a little inlet.

Out of it stepped a man of medium height, wearing a Tartar sheepskin cap. He waved, and all three set to work to drag something out of the boat. The cargo was so large that, to this day, I cannot understand how it was that the boat did not sink.

Each of them shouldered a bundle, and they set off along the shore. I soon lost sight of them.

I had to return to my quarters, but I confess I was rendered so uneasy by all these strange happenings that I found it hard to await the morning.

My Cossack was very much astonished when, on waking up, he saw me fully dressed. I did not, however, tell him the reason. For some time I stood at the window, admiring the blue sky studded with wisps of cloud and the distant shore of the Crimea, stretching out in a lilac-colored streak and ending in a cliff, on the summit of which the white lighthouse gleamed.

Then I went to Fort Phanagoriya, to ascertain from the Commandant at what hour I should depart for Gelenjik.

But the Commandant, alas, could not give me any definite information. The vessels lying in the harbor were either patrol boats or merchant ships which had not yet even begun to take in cargo.

"Maybe in about three or four days' time a mail boat will come in," said the Commandant, "and then we shall see."

I returned to the hut sulky and wrathful. My Cossack met me at the door with a frightened countenance.

"Things are looking bad, sir!" he said.

"Yes, my friend; Heaven knows when we shall get away!"

Hereupon he became still more uneasy, and, bending towards me, he said in a whisper:

"This is a strange place! I met a sergeant from the Black Sea today — he's an acquaintance of mine — he was in my detachment last year. When I told him where we were staying, he said, 'That place is uncanny, old fellow; they're wicked people there!' . . . . And, indeed, what sort of a blind boy is that? He goes everywhere alone, to fetch water and to buy bread at the bazaar. It is evident they have become accustomed to that sort of thing here."

"Well, what then? Tell me, though, has the mistress of the place put in an appearance?"

118

"During your absence today, an old woman and her daughter arrived."

"What daughter? She has no daughter!"

"Heaven knows who it can be, if it isn't her daughter; but the old woman is sitting over there in the hut right now."

I entered the hovel. A blazing fire was burning in the stove, and they were cooking a dinner which struck me as being a rather luxurious one for poor people. To all my questions the old woman replied that she was deaf and could not hear me. I couldn't get any information from her.

I turned to the blind boy who was sitting in front of the stove, putting twigs into the fire. "Now, then, you little blind devil," I said, taking him by the ear. "Tell me, where were you roaming with the bundle last night, eh?"

The blind boy suddenly burst out weeping, shrieking and wailing. "Where did I go? I did not go anywhere . . . with the bundle? . . . what bundle?"

This time the old woman heard, and she began to mutter, "Listen to them plot, and against a poor crippled boy too! What are you touching him for? What has he done to you?"

I had enough of this, and went out, firmly resolved to find the key to the riddle.

I wrapped myself up in my felt cloak and, sitting down on a rock by the fence, gazed into the distance. Before me stretched the sea, still agitated by the storm of the previous night, and its monotonous roar, like the murmur of a town over which slumber is beginning to creep, recalled bygone years to my mind. My thoughts were transported northward to our cold capital. Disturbed by my recollections, I became oblivious to my surroundings.

About an hour passed thus, perhaps even longer. Suddenly something resembling a song struck upon my ear. It was indeed a song, and the voice was a woman's, young and fresh — but where was it coming from? . . . I listened; it was a harmonious melody — now slow and plaintive, now swift and lively. I looked around me — there was nobody to be seen. I listened again — the sounds seemed to be falling from the sky.

I raised my eyes. On the roof of my cabin stood a young woman in a striped dress, with her hair hanging loose — a regular water nymph. Shading her eyes from the sun's rays with the palm of her hand, she was gazing intently into the distance. At one time, she would laugh and talk to herself; at another, she would strike up her song anew.

I have retained that song in my memory, word for word:

At their own free will
They seem to wander
O'er the green sea yonder,
Those ships, as still
They are onward going,
With white sails flowing.
And among those ships
My eye can mark
My own dear bark:
By two oars guided
(All unprovided
With sails) it slips.
The storm-wind raves:
And the old ships — see!
With wings spread free,
Over the waves
They scatter and flee!
The sea I will hail
With obeisance deep:
"Thou base one, hark!
Thou must not fail
My little bark
From harm to keep!"
For lo! 'tis bearing
Most precious gear,
And brave and daring
The arms that steer
Within the dark
My little bark.

Involuntarily the thought occurred to me that I had heard the same voice the night before. I reflected for a moment, and when I looked up at the roof again, there was no one to be seen. Suddenly she darted past me, with another song on her lips, and, snapping her fingers, she ran up to the old woman. A quarrel arose between them. The old woman grew angry, and the girl laughed loudly.

Then I saw my Undine running and skipping again. She came up to where I was, stopped, and gazed fixedly into my face as if surprised at my presence. Then she turned carelessly away and went quietly towards the harbor.

But this was not all. The whole day she kept hovering around my lodging, singing and skipping without a moment's interruption.

Strange creature! There was not the slightest sign of insanity in her face. On the contrary, her eyes, which were continually resting upon me, were bright and piercing. Moreover, they seemed to be endowed with a certain magnetic power, and each time they looked at me they appeared to be expecting a question. But I had only to open my lips to speak, and away she would run, with a sly smile.

Certainly never before had I seen a woman like her. She was by no means beautiful; but, as in other matters, I have my own ideas on the subject of beauty. There was a good deal of breeding in her.

Breeding in women, as in horses, is a great thing: a discovery, the credit of which belongs to young France. It — that is to say, breeding, not young France — is chiefly to be detected in the gait, in the hands and feet; the nose, in particular, is of the greatest significance. In Russia a straight nose is rarer than a small foot.

My songstress appeared to be not more than eighteen years of age. The unusual suppleness of her figure, the characteristic and original way she had of inclining her head, her long, light-brown hair, the golden sheen of her slightly sunburnt neck and shoulders, and especially her straight nose — all these held me fascinated. Although in her sidelong glances I could read a certain wildness and disdain, although in her smile there was a certain vagueness, yet — such is the force of predilections — that straight nose of hers drove me crazy. I fancied that I had found Goethe's Mignon — that queer creature of his German imagination. And, indeed, there was a good deal of similarity between them; the same rapid transitions from the utmost restlessness to complete immobility, the same enigmatic speeches, the same gambols, the same strange songs.

Towards evening I stopped her at the door and entered into the following conversation with her.

"Tell me, my beauty," I asked, "what were you doing on the roof today?"

"I was looking to see from what direction the wind was blowing."

"What did you want to know that for?"

"Whence the wind blows comes happiness."

"Well? Were you invoking happiness with your song?"

"Where there is singing there is also happiness."

"But what if your song were to bring sorrow?"

"Well, what then? Where things won't be better, they will be worse; and from bad to good again is not far."

"And who taught you that song?"

"Nobody taught me; it comes into my head and I sing. Whoever is to hear it, he will hear it, and whoever ought not to hear it, he will not understand it."

"What is your name, my songstress?"

"He who baptized me knows."

"And who baptized you?"

"How should I know?"

"What a secretive girl you are! But look here, I have learned something about you" — she neither changed countenance nor moved her lips, as though my discovery was of no concern to her — "I have learned that you went to the shore last night."

And, thereupon, I very gravely retailed to her all that I had seen, thinking that I would embarrass her. Not a bit of it! She burst out laughing heartily.

"You have seen much, but know little; and what you do know, see that you keep it under lock and key."

"But suppose I was to take it into my head to inform the Commandant?" and here I assumed a very serious, not to say stern, demeanor.

She gave a sudden start, began to sing, and disappeared like a bird frightened out of a thicket. My last words were altogether out of place. I had no suspicion then how momentous they were, but afterwards I had occasion to rue them.

As soon as the dusk of evening fell, I ordered the Cossack to heat the teapot, campaign fashion. I lit a candle and sat down by the table, smoking my traveling-pipe.

I was just about to finish my second glass of tea, when suddenly the door creaked, and I heard behind me the sound of footsteps and the light rustle of a dress. I started and turned around. It was she — my Undine. Softly and without saying a word, she sat down opposite to me and fixed her eyes upon me. Her glance seemed wondrously tender, I know not why; it reminded me of those glances which, in years gone by, so despotically played with my life. She seemed to be waiting for a question, but I kept silent, filled with an inexplicable sense of embarrassment. Mental agitation was revealed by the dull pallor which overspread her countenance. Her hand, which I noticed was trembling slightly, moved aimlessly about the table. At one time her breast heaved, and at another she seemed to be holding her breath.

This little comedy was beginning to pall upon me, and I was about to break the silence in a most prosaic manner (that is, by offering her a glass of tea) when suddenly springing up, she threw her arms around my neck and pressed her moist, fiery lips upon mine. Darkness swept over my eyes; my head began to swim. I embraced her with the whole strength of youthful passion. But, like a snake, she glided from between my arms, whispering in my ear as she did so:

"Tonight, when everyone is asleep, go out to the shore."

Like an arrow she sprang from the room. In the hall she upset the teapot and a candle which was standing on the floor.

"Little devil!" cried the Cossack, who had settled himself on the straw and had contemplated warming himself with the rest of the tea. It was only then that I recovered my senses.

In about two hours' time, when all had grown silent in the harbor, I awakened my Cossack. "If I fire a pistol," I said, "run to the shore."

He stared open-eyed and answered mechanically, "Very well, sir."

I stuffed a pistol in my belt and went out. She was waiting for me at the edge of the cliff. Her attire was more than light, and a small kerchief girded her supple waist.

"Follow me!" she said, taking me by the hand, and we began to descend.

I cannot understand how it was that I did not break my neck. Down below we turned to the right and took the path along which I had followed the blind boy the evening before. The moon had not yet risen, and only two little stars, like two guardian lighthouses, were twinkling in the dark blue vault of heaven. The heavy waves, with measured and even motion, rolled one after the other, scarcely lifting the solitary boat which was moored to the shore.

"Let us get into the boat," said my companion.

I hesitated. I am no lover of sentimental trips on the sea; but this was not the time to draw back. She leaped into the boat, and I after her; and I had not time to recover my wits before I observed that we were adrift.

"What is the meaning of this?" I said angrily.

"It means," she answered, making me sit on the bench and throwing her arms around my waist, "it means that I love you!"

Her cheek was pressed close to mine and I felt her burning breath upon my face. Suddenly something fell noisily into the water. I clutched at my belt — my pistol was gone! Ah, now a terrible suspicion crept into my soul, and the blood rushed to my head! I looked around. We were about three hundred feet from the shore, and I could not swim a stroke! I tried to thrust her away from me, but she clung like a cat to my clothes, and suddenly a violent wrench all but threw me into the sea. The boat rocked, but I recovered my balance, and a desperate struggle began.

Fury lent me strength, but I soon found that I was no match for my opponent in agility.

"What do you want?" I cried, firmly squeezing her little hands.

Her fingers crunched, but her serpentine nature bore up against the torture, and she did not utter a cry.

"You saw us," she answered. "You will tell on us."

And, with a supernatural effort, she flung me to the side of the boat; we both hung half overboard; her hair touched the water. The decisive moment had come. I planted my knee against the bottom of the boat, caught her by the tresses with one hand and by the throat with the other; she let go of my clothes, and, in an instant, I had thrown her into the waves.

It was now rather dark; once or twice her head appeared for an instant amidst the sea foam, and then I saw no more of her.

I found half of an old oar at the bottom of the boat, and somehow, after lengthy efforts, I made it back to land. Making my way along the shore towards the hut, I happened to gaze in the direction of the spot where, on the previous night, the blind boy had awaited the nocturnal mariner. The moon was already rolling through the sky, and it seemed to me that somebody in white was sitting on the shore.

Spurred by curiosity, I crept up and crouched down in the grass on the top of the cliff. By thrusting my head out a little way I was able to get a good view of everything that was happening down below. I was not very much astonished, but almost rejoiced, when I recognized my water nymph. She was wringing the seafoam from her long hair. Her wet garment outlined her supple figure and her high bosom.

Soon a boat appeared in the distance; it drew near rapidly; and, as on the night before, a man in a Tartar cap stepped out of it, but he now had his hair cropped round in the Cossack fashion, and a large knife was sticking out behind his leather belt.

"Yanko," the girl said, "all is lost!"

Then their conversation continued, but so softly that I could not catch a word of it.

"But where is the blind boy?" said Yanko at last, raising his voice.

"I told him to come," was the reply.

After a few minutes the blind boy appeared, dragging on his back a sack, which they placed in the boat.

"Listen!" said Yanko to the blind boy. "Guard that place! You know where I mean? There are valuable goods there. Tell" — I could not catch the name — "that I can no longer work for him. Things have gone badly. He will see me no more. It is dangerous now. I will look for work elsewhere. He will never be able to find another daredevil like me. Tell him also that if he had paid me a little better for my labors, I would not have forsaken him. For me there is always a path, wherever the wind blows and the sea roars."

After a short silence Yanko continued: "She is coming with me. It is impossible for her to remain here. Tell the old woman that it is time for her to die; she has been here a long time, and the line must be drawn somewhere. As for us, she will never see us anymore."

"And I?" said the blind boy in a plaintive voice.

"What use have I for you?" was the answer.

In the meantime my Undine had sprung into the boat. She beckoned to her companion with her hand. He placed something in the blind boy's hand and added:

"There, buy yourself some gingerbread."

"Is this all?" said the blind boy.

"Well, here is some more." The money fell and jingled, as it struck the rock. The blind boy did not pick it up.

Yanko took his seat in the boat; the wind was blowing from the shore; they hoisted the little sail and sped rapidly away. For a long time the white sail gleamed in the moonlight amid the dark waves.

Still the blind boy remained seated upon the shore, and then I heard something which sounded like sobbing. The boy was, in fact, weeping, and for a long, long time his tears flowed . . . I grew heavy-hearted. For what reason should fate have thrown me into the peaceful circle of honorable smugglers? Like a stone cast into smooth water, I had disturbed their quietude, and I had barely escaped going to the bottom like a stone.

I returned to my quarters. In the hall the burnt-out candle was spluttering on a wooden platter, and my Cossack, contrary to orders, was fast asleep, with his rifle held in both hands. I left him at rest, took the candle, and entered the hut. Alas! my money box, my sabre with the silver chasing, my Daghe-stan dagger — the gift of a friend — all had vanished! It was then that I guessed what articles the cursed blind boy had been dragging along.

Roughly shaking the Cossack, I woke him up and scolded him in a bad-tempered rage. But what was there to do? Would it not have been ridiculous to complain to the authorities that I had been robbed by a blind boy and all but drowned by an eighteen-year-old girl?

Thank heaven, an opportunity to get away presented itself in the morning, and I left Taman. What became of the old woman and the poor blind boy I know not. And, besides, what are the joys and sorrows of mankind to me — me, a traveling officer, and one, moreover, on government business to obtain horses for the post?

Touch and Go—A Midshipman's Story

Arthur Conan Doyle

First published in *Cassell's Family Magazine*, April 1886; First book appearance -- *The Unknown Conan Doyle*, 1929

What is there in all nature which is more beautiful or more inspiriting than the sight of the great ocean, when a merry breeze sweeps over it, and the sun glints down upon the long green ridges with their crests of snow? Sad indeed must be the heart which does not respond to the cheery splashing of the billows and their roar upon the shingle. There are times, however, when the great heaving giant is in another and a darker mood. Those who, like myself, have been tossed upon the dark waters through a long night, while the great waves spat their foam over them in their fury, and the fierce winds howled above them, will ever after look upon the sea with other eyes. However peaceful it may be, they will see the lurking fiend beneath its smiling surface. It is a great wild beast of uncertain temper and incalculable strength.

Once, and once only, during the long years which I have spent at sea, have I found myself at the mercy of this monster. There were circumstances, too, upon that occasion, which threatened a more terrible catastrophe than the loss of my own single life. I have set myself to write down, as concisely and as accurately as I can, the facts in connection with that adventure and its very remarkable consequences.

In 1868 I was a lad of fourteen, and had just completed my first voyage in the *Paraguay*, one of the finest vessels of the finest of the Pacific lines, in which I was a midshipman. On reaching Liverpool, our ship had been laid up for a month or so, and I had obtained leave of absence to visit my relations, who were living on the banks of the Clyde. I hurried north with all the eagerness of a boy who has been abroad for the first time, and met with a loving reception from my parents and from my only sister. I have never known any pleasure in life which could compare with that which these reunions bring to a lad whose disposition is affectionate.

The little village at which my family were living was called Rudmore, and was situated in one of the most beautiful spots in the whole of the Clyde. Indeed, it was the natural advantages of its situation which had induced my father to purchase a villa there. Our grounds ran down to the water's edge, and included a small wooden jetty which projected into the river. Beside this jetty was anchored a small yacht, which had belonged to the former proprietor, and which had been included in the rest of the property when purchased by my father. She was a smart little clipper of about three-ton burden, and directly my eyes fell upon her I determined that I would test her sea-going qualities.

My sister had a younger friend of hers, Maud Sumter, staying with her at this time, and the three of us made frequent excursions about the country, and occasionally put out into the Firth in order to fish. On all these nautical expeditions we were accompanied by an old fisherman named Jock Reid, in whom my father had confidence. At first we were rather glad to have the old man's company, and were amused by his garrulous chat and strange reminiscences. After a time, however, we began to resent the idea of having a guardian placed over us, and the grievance weighed with double stress upon me, for, midshipman-like, I had fallen a victim to the blue-eyes and golden hair of my sister's pretty playmate, and I conceived that without our boatman I might have many an opportunity of showing my gallantry and my affection. Besides, it seemed a monstrous thing that a real sailor, albeit only fourteen years of age, who had actually been round Cape Horn, should not be trusted with the command of a boat in a quiet Scottish firth. We put our three youthful heads together over the matter, and the result was a unanimous determination to mutiny against our ancient commander.

It was not difficult to carry our resolution into practice. One bright winter's day, when the sun was shining cheerily, but a stiffish breeze was ruffling the surface of the water, we announced our intention of going for a sail, and Jock Reid was as usual summoned from his cottage to escort us. I remember that the old man looked very doubtfully at the glass in my father's hall, and then at the eastern sky, in which the clouds were piling up into a gigantic cumulus.

"Ye maunna gang far the day," he said, shaking his grizzled head. "It's like to blow hard afore evening."

"No, no, Jock," we cried in chorus; "we don't want to go far."

The old sailor came down with us to the boat, still grumbling his presentiments about the coming weather. I stalked along with all the dignity of chief conspirator, while my sister and Maud followed expectantly, full of timidity and admiration for my audacity. When we reached the boat I helped the boatman to set the mainsail and the jib, and he was about to cast her off from her moorings when I played the card which I had been reserving.

"Jock," I said, slipping a shilling into his hand; "I'm afraid you'll feel it cold when we get out. You had better get yourself a drop of something before we start."

"Indeed I will, maister," said Jock emphatically. "I'm no as young as I was, and the coffee keeps the cold out."

"You run up to the house," I said; "we can wait until you come back."

Poor old Jock, suspecting no treachery, made off in the direction of the village, and was soon out of sight. The instant he had disappeared six busy little

138

hands were at work undoing the moorings, and in less than a minute we were clear of the land, and were shooting gallantly out into the centre of the Firth of Clyde. Under her press of canvas, the little boat heeled over until her lee-gunwale was level with the water, and as we plunged into the waves the spray came showering over the bows and splashing on our deck. Far away on the beach we could see old Jock, who had been warned by the villagers of our flight, running eagerly up and down, and waving his arms in his excitement. How we laughed at the old man's impotent anger, and what fun we made of the salt foam which wet our faces and sprinkled on our lips! We sang, we romped, we played, and when we tired of this the two girls sat in the sheets, while I held the tiller and told many stories of my nautical experiences, and of the incidents of my one and only voyage.

At first we were somewhat undecided as to what course we should steer, or where we should make for; but after consultation it was unanimously decided that we should run out to the mouth of the Firth. Old Jock had always avoided the open sea, and had beaten about in the river, so it seemed to us, now that we had deposed our veteran commander, that it was a favourable opportunity for showing what we could do without him. The wind, too, was blowing from the eastward, and therefore was favourable to the attempt. We pulled the mainsail as square as possible, and keeping the tiller steady, ran rapidly before the wind in the direction of the sea.

Behind us the great cumulus of clouds had lengthened and broadened, but the sun was still shining brightly, making the crests of the waves sparkle again, like long ridges of fire. The banks of the Firth, which are four or five miles apart, are well wooded, and many a lovely villa and stately castle peeped out from among the trees as we swept past. Far behind us we saw the long line of smoke which told where Greenock and Glasgow lay, with their toiling thousands of inhabitants. In front rose a great stately mountain-peak, that of Goatfell, in Arran, with the clouds wreathed coquettishly round the summit. Away to the north, too, in the purple distance lay ranges of mountains stretching along the whole horizon, and throwing strange shadows as the bright rays of the sun fell upon their rugged sides.

We were not lonely as we made our way down the great artery which carries the commerce of the west of Scotland to the sea. Boats of all sizes and shapes passed and re-passed us. Eager little steamers went panting by with their loads of Glasgow citizens, going to or returning from the great city. Yachts and launches, and fishing-boats, came and went in every direction. One of the latter crossed our bows, and one of her crew, a rough-bearded fellow, shouted hoarsely at us; but the wind prevented us from hearing what he said. As we neared the sea a great Atlantic steamer went slowly past us, with her big yellow funnel vomiting forth clouds of smoke, and her whistle blowing to warn the smaller craft to keep out of her way. Her passengers lined the side to watch us as we shot past them, very proud of our little boat and of ourselves.

We had brought some sandwiches away with us, and a bottle of milk, so that there was no reason why we should shorten our cruise. We stood on accordingly until we were abreast of Ardrossan, which is at the mouth of the river and exactly opposite to the island of Arran, which lies in the open sea. The strait across is about eight miles in width, and my two companions were both clamorous that we should cross.

"It looks very stormy," I said, glancing at the pile of clouds behind us; "I think we had better put back."

"Oh, do let us go on to Arran!" little Maud cried enthusiastically.

"Do, Archie," echoed my sister; "surely, you are not afraid?"

To tell the truth, I *was* afraid, for I read the signs of the weather better than they did. The reproachful look in Maud's blue eyes at what she took to be my faint-heartedness overcame all my prudence.

"If you wish to go, we'll go," I said; and we sailed out from the mouth of the river into the strait.

Hitherto we had been screened from the wind to some extent by the hills behind us, but as we emerged from our shelter it came upon us in fiercer and more prolonged blasts. The mast bent like a

whip under the pressure upon the sail, and would, I
believe, have snapped short off, had it not been
that I had knowledge enough of sailing to be able to
take in a couple of reefs in the great sail. Even then
the boat lay over in an alarming manner, so that we
had to hold on to the weather bulwarks to prevent
our slipping off. The waves, too, were much larger
than they had been in the Firth, and we shipped so
much water that I had to bail it out several times
with my hat. The girls clapped their hands and cried
out with delight as the water came over us, but I
was grave because I knew the danger; and seeing
me grave, they became grave too. Ahead of us the
great mountain-peak towered up into the clouds,
with green woods clustering about its base; and we
could see the houses along the beach, and the long
shining strip of yellow sand. Behind us the dark
clouds became darker, lined at the base with the
peculiar lurid tint which is nature's danger signal. It
was evident that the breeze would soon become a
gale, and a violent one. We should not lose a
moment in getting back to the river, and I already
bitterly repented that I had ever left its sheltering
banks.

We put the boat round with all the speed we could,
but it was no light task for three children. When at
last we began to tack for the Scotch coast, we
realised how difficult a matter it was for us to return.
As long as we went with the wind, we went also
with the waves; and it was only a stray one which
broke over us. The moment, however, that we
turned our broadside towards the sea we were

deluged with water, which poured in faster than we could bail it out. A jagged flash of lightning clove the dark eastern sky, followed by a deafening peal of thunder. It was clear that the gale was about to burst; and it was evident to me that if it caught us in our present position we should infallibly be swamped. With much difficulty we squared our sail once more, and ran before the wind. It had veered a couple of points to the north, so that our course promised to take us to the south of the island. We shipped less water now than before, but on the other hand, every minute drove us out into the wild Irish Sea, further and further from home.

It was blowing so hard by this time, and the waters made such a clashing, that it was hard to hear each other's words. Little Maudie nestled at my side, and took my hand in hers. My sister clung to the rail at the other side of me.

"Don't you think," she said, "that we could sail right into one of the harbours in Arran? I know there is a harbour at Brodick, which is just opposite us."

"We had better keep away from it altogether," I said. "We should be sure to be wrecked if we got near the coast; and it is just as bad to be wrecked there as in the open sea."

"Where are we going?" she cried.

"Anywhere the wind takes us," I answered; "it is our only chance. Don't cry, Maudie; we'll get back all right when the storm is over." I tried to comfort them, for they were both in tears; and, indeed, I could hardly keep my sobs down myself, for I was a very little fellow to be placed in such a position.

As the storm came down on us it became so dark that we could hardly see the island in front of us, and the dark line of the Bute coast. We flew through the water at a tremendous pace, skimming over the great seething waves, while the wind howled and screamed through our rigging as though the whole air was full of pursuing fiends intent upon our destruction. The two girls cowered, shivering with terror, at the bottom of the boat, while I endeavoured to comfort them as well as I could, and to keep our craft before the wind. As the evening drew in and we increased our distance from the shore; the gale grew in power. The great dark waves towered high above our mast-head, so that when we lay in the trough of the sea, we saw nothing but the sombre liquid walls in front and behind us. Then we would sweep up the black slope, till from the summit we could see a dreary prospect of raging waters around us, and then we would sink down, down into the valley upon the other side. It was only the extreme lightness and buoyancy of our little craft which saved her from instant destruction. A dozen times a gigantic billow would curl over our heads, as though it were about to break over us, but each time the gallant boat rose triumphantly over it, shaking herself after each collision with the waters as a seabird might trim her feathers.

Never shall I forget the horrors of that night! As the darkness settled down upon us, we saw the loom of a great rock some little distance from us, and we knew that we were passing Ailsa Craig. In one sense it was a relief to us to know that it was behind us, because there was now no land which we need fear, but only the great expanse of the Irish Sea. In the short intervals when the haze lifted, we could see the twinkling lights from the Scottish lighthouses glimmering through the darkness behind us. The waves had been terrible in the daytime, but they were worse now. It was better to see them towering over us than to hear them hissing and seething far above our heads, and to be able to make out nothing except the occasional gleam of a line of foam. Once, and once only, the moon disentangled itself from the thick hurrying clouds which obscured its face. Then we caught a glimpse of a great wilderness of foaming, tossing waters, but the dark scud drifted over the sky, and the silvery light faded away until all was gloom once more.

What a long weary night it was! Cold and hungry, and shivering with terror, the three of us clung together, peering out into the darkness and praying as none of us had ever prayed before. During all the long hours we still tore through the waters to the south and west, for the wind was now blowing from the north-east. As the day dawned, grey and cheerless, we saw the rugged coast of Ireland lining the whole western horizon. And now it was, in the first dim light of dawn, that our great misfortune occurred to us. Whether it was the result of the long-continued strain, or whether some gust of particular violence had caught the sail, we have never known, but suddenly there was a sharp cracking, rending noise, and next moment our mast was trailing over the side, with the rigging and the sails flapping on the surface of the water. At the same instant, our momentum being checked, a great sea broke over the boat and nearly swamped us. Fortunately the blow was so great, that it drove our boat round so that her head came to the seas once more. I bailed frantically with my cap, for she was half full of water, and I knew a little more would sink her, but as fast as I threw the water out, more came surging in. It was at this moment, when all seemed lost to us, that I heard my sister give a joyful cry, and looking up, saw a large steam launch ploughing its way towards us through the storm. Then the tears which I had restrained so long came to my relief, and I broke down completely in the reaction which came upon us, when we knew that we were saved.

It was no easy matter for our preservers to rescue us, for close contact between the two little craft was dangerous to both. A rope was thrown to us, however, and willing hands at the other end drew us one after the other to a place of safety. Maudie had fainted, and my sister and I were so weakened by cold and fatigue, that we were carried helpless to the cabin of the launch, where we were given some hot soup, after which we fell asleep, in spite of the rolling and tossing of the little vessel.

How long we slept I have no idea, but when we woke it appeared to be considerably past mid-day. My sister and Maudie were in the bunk opposite, and I could see that they were still sleeping. A tall, dark-bearded man was stooping over a chart which was pinned down to the table, measuring out distances with a pair of compasses. When I moved he glanced up and saw that I was awake.

"Well, mate," he said cheerily, "how are you now?"

"All right," I said; "thanks to you."

"It was touch and go," he remarked. "She foundered within five minutes of your coming aboard. Have you any idea where you are now?"

"No," I said.

"You're just off the Isle of Man. We're going to land you there on the west coast, where no one is likely to see us. We've had to go out of our course to do it, and I should have preferred to have taken you on to France, but the master thinks you should be sent home as soon as possible."

"Why don't you want to be seen?" I asked, leaning on my elbow.

"Never mind," he said; "we don't—and that's enough. Besides, you and these girls must keep quiet about us when you land. You must say that a fishing-boat saved you."

"All right," I said. I was much surprised at the earnestness with which the man made the request.

What sort of vessel was this that we had got aboard of? A smuggler, perhaps, certainly something illegal, or else why this anxiety not to be seen? Yet they had been kind and good to us, so whatever they might be, it was not for us to expose them. As I lay speculating upon the point I heard a sudden bustle upon deck, and a head looked down the hatchway.

"There's a vessel ahead of us that looks like a gun-boat," it said.

The captain—for such I presumed the dark-haired man to be—dropped his compasses, and rushed upon deck. A moment later he came down, evidently much excited.

"Come on," he said; "we must get rid of you at once." He woke the girls up, and the three of us were hurried to the side and into a boat, which was manned by a couple of sailors. The hilly coast of the island was not more than a hundred or two yards away. As I passed into the boat, a middle-aged man, in dark clothes and a grey overcoat, laid his hand upon my shoulder.

"Remember," he said—"silence! You might do much harm!"

"Not a word," I answered.

He waved an adieu to us as our oarsmen bent to their oars, and in a few minutes we found our feet once more upon dry land. The boat pulled rapidly back, and then we saw the launch shoot away southward, evidently to avoid a large ship which was steaming down in the distance. When we looked again she was a mere dot on the waters, and from that day to this we have never seen or heard anything of our deliverers.

I fortunately had money enough in my pocket to send a telegram to my father, and then we put up at a hotel at Douglas, until he came himself to fetch us away. Fear and suspense had whitened his hair; but he was repaid for all when he saw us once more, and clasped us in his arms. He even forgot, in his delight, to scold us for the piece of treachery which had originated our misfortunes; and not the least hearty greeting which we received upon our return to the banks of the Clyde was from old Jock himself, who had quite forgiven us our desertion.

And who were our deliverers? That is a somewhat difficult question to answer, and yet I have an idea of their identity. Within a few days of our return, all England was ringing with the fact that Stephens, the famous Fenian head-centre, had made good his escape to the Continent. It may be that I am weaving a romance out of very commonplace material; but it has often seemed to me that if that gun-boat had overtaken that launch, it is quite possible that the said Mr. Stephens might never have put in an appearance upon the friendly shores of France. Be his politics what they may, if our deliverer really was Mr. Stephens, he was a good friend to us in our need, and we often look back with gratitude to our short acquaintance with the passenger in the grey coat.

21st Century Note: James Stephens was a political activist and revolutionary who worked to end British rule in Ireland, especially after Ireland was devastated in the 1840's by famine and severe taxation. He traveled to France on at least one occasion to avoid arrest.

Circumstances in Connection with the SS Californian—
(An excerpt from the official 1912 British investigation into the sinking of the Titanic)

It is here necessary to consider the circumstances relating to the s.s. "Californian."

On the 14th of April, the s.s. "Californian" of the Leyland line, Mr. Stanley Lord, Master, was on her passage from London, which port she left on April 5th, to Boston, U.S., were [sic] she subsequently arrived on April 19th. She was a vessel of 6,223 tons gross and 4,038 net. Her full speed was 12 1/2 to 13 knots. She had a passenger certificate, but was not carrying any passengers at the time. She belonged to the International Mercantile Marine Company, the owners of the "Titanic."

At 7.30 p.m., ship's time, on 14th April, a wireless message was sent from this ship to the "Antillian." (Evans, 8941, 8943)

"To Captain, 'Antillian,' 6.30 p.m., apparent ship's time, lat. 42° 3' N., long. 49° 9' W. Three large bergs, 5 miles to southward of us. Regards. - Lord."

The message was intercepted by the "Titanic," and when the Marconi operator (Evans) of the "Californian" offered this ice report to the Marconi operator of the "Titanic," shortly after 7.30 p.m., the latter replied, "It is all right. I heard you sending it to the 'Antillian,' and I have got it." (8972) (Lord, 6710)

The "Californian" proceeded on her course S. 89° W. true until 10.20 p.m. ship's time, when she was obliged to stop and reverse engines because she was running into field ice, which stretched as far as could then be seen to the northward and southward.

The Master told the Court that he made her position at that time to be 42° 5' N., 57° 7' W. (6704) This position is recorded in the log book, which was written up from the scrap log book by the Chief Officer. The scrap log is destroyed. It is a position about 19 miles N. by E. of the position of the "Titanic" when she foundered, and is said to have been fixed by dead reckoning and verified by observations. I am satisfied that this position is not accurate. The Master "twisted her head" to E.N.E. by the compass and she remained approximately stationary until 5.15 a.m. on the following morning. The ship was slowly swinging round to starboard during the night. (6713) (Groves, 8249)

At about 11 p.m. a steamer's light was seen approaching from the eastward. The Master went to Evans' room and asked, "What ships he had." The latter replied: "I think the 'Titanic' is near us. I have got her." (Evans, 8962, 8988) The Master said: "You had better advise the 'Titanic' we are stopped and surrounded by ice." This Evans did, calling up the "Titanic" and sending: "We are stopped and surrounded by ice." (8993) The "Titanic" replied: "Keep out." The "Titanic" was in communication with Cape Race, which station was then sending messages to her. (8994) The reason why the "Titanic" answered, "Keep out," (9004) was that her Marconi operator could not hear what Cape Race was saying, as from her proximity, the message from the "Californian" was much stronger than any message being taken in by the "Titanic" from Cape Race, which was much further off. (9022) Evans heard the "Titanic" continuing to communicate with Cape Race up to the time he turned in at 11.30 p.m.

The Master of the "Californian" states that when observing the approaching steamer as she got nearer, he saw more lights, a few deck lights, and also her green side light. He considered that at 11 o'clock she was approximately six or seven miles away, and at some time between 11 and 11.30, he first saw her green light, she was then about 5 miles off. (Lord, 6761) He noticed then about 11.30 she stopped. In his opinion this steamer was of about the same size as the "Californian"; a medium-sized steamer, "something like ourselves." (6752)

From the evidence of Mr. Groves, third officer of the "Californian," who was the officer of the first watch, it would appear that the Master was not actually on the bridge when the steamer was sighted.

Mr. Groves made out two masthead lights; the steamer was changing her bearing slowly as she got closer, (Groves, 8147) and as she approached he went to the chart room and reported this to the

Master; he added, "she is evidently a passenger steamer." (8174) In fact, Mr. Groves never appears to have had any doubt on this subject: In answer to a question during his examination, "Had she much light?" he said, "Yes, a lot of light. There was absolutely no doubt of her being a passenger steamer, at least in my mind." (8178)

Gill, the assistant donkeyman of the "Californian," who was on deck at midnight said, referring to this steamer: "It could not have been anything but a passenger boat, she was to [sic] large." (Gill, 18136)

By the evidence Mr. Groves, the Master, in reply to his report, said: "Call her up on the Morse lamp, and see if you can get any answer." This he proceeded to do. The Master came up and joined him on the bridge and remarked: "That does not look like a passenger steamer." (Groves, 8197) Mr. Groves replied "It is, sir. When she stopped, her lights seemed to go out, and I suppose they have been put out for the night." (8203) Mr. Groves states that these lights went out at 11.40, and remembers that time because "one bell was struck to call the middle watch." (8217) The Master did not join him on the bridge until shortly afterwards, and consequently after the steamer had stopped.

In his examination Mr. Groves admitted that if this steamer's head was turning to port after she stopped, it might account for the diminution of lights, by many of them being shut out. Her steaming lights were still visible and also her port side light. (8228)

The Captain only remained upon the bridge for a few minutes. (8241) In his evidence he stated that Mr. Groves had made no observations to him about the steamer's deck lights going out. (Lord, 6866) Mr. Groves' Morse signalling appears to have been ineffectual (although at one moment he thought he was being answered), and he gave it up. He remained on the bridge until relieved by Mr. Stone, the second officer, just after midnight. In turning the "Californian" over to him, he pointed out the steamer and said: "she has been stopped since 11.40; she is a passenger steamer. At about the moment she stopped she put her lights out." (Stone, 7810) When Mr. Groves was in the witness-box the following questions were put to him by me: -

"Speaking as an experienced seaman and knowing what you do know now, do you think that steamer that you know was throwing up rockets, and that you say was a passenger steamer, was the 'Titanic'? - Do I think it? Yes? - From what I have heard subsequently? Yes? - Most decidedly I do, but I do not put myself as being an experienced man. But that is your opinion as far as your experience goes? - Yes, it is, my Lord."

(Groves, 8441)

Mr. Stone states that the Master, who was also up (but apparently not on the bridge), pointed out the steamer to him with instructions to tell him if her bearings altered or if she got any closer; he also stated that Mr. Groves had called her up on the Morse lamp and had received no reply. (Stone, 7815)

Mr. Stone had with him during the middle watch an apprentice named Gibson, whose attention was first drawn to the steamer's lights at about 12.20 a.m. (Gibson, 7424) He could see a masthead light, her red light (with glasses) and a "glare of white lights on her after deck." He first thought her masthead light was flickering and next thought it was a Morse light, "calling us up." (7443) He replied, but could not get into communication, and finally came to the conclusion that it was, as he had first supposed, the masthead light flickering. Some time after 12.30 a.m., Gill, the donkeyman, states that he saw two rockets fired from the ship which he had been observing, (Gill, 18156-61) and about 1.10 a.m., Mr. Stone reported to the Captain by voice pipe, they he had seen five white rockets from the direction of the steamer. (Stone, 7870) He states that the Master answered, "Are they Company's signals?" and that he replied, "I do not know, but they appear to me to be white rockets." The Master told him to "go on Morsing," and, when he received any information, to send the apprentice down to him with it. (7879) Gibson states that Mr. Stone informed him that he had reported to the Master, and that the Master had said the steamer was to be called up by Morse light. (Gibson, 7479) This witness thinks the time was 12.55; he at once proceeded again to call the steamer up by Morse. He got no reply, but the vessel fired three more white rockets; these rockets were also seen by Mr. Stone.

Both Mr. Stone and the apprentice kept the steamer under observation, looking at her from time to time with their glasses. Between 1 o'clock and 1.40 some conversation passed between them. Mr. Stone remarked to Gibson: "Look at her now, she looks very queer out of water, her lights look queer." (7515) He also is said by Gibson to have remarked, "A ship is not going to fire rockets at sea for nothing;" (7529) and admits himself that he may possibly have used that expression. (Stone, 7894)

Mr. Stone states that he saw the last of the rockets fired at about 1.40, and after watching the steamer for some twenty minutes more he sent Gibson down to the Master.

"I told Gibson to go down to the Master, and be sure to wake him, and tell him that altogether we had seen eight of these white lights like white rockets in the direction of this other steamer; that this steamer was disappearing in the southwest, that we had called her up repeatedly on the Morse lamp and received no information whatsoever."

Gibson states that he went down to the chart room and told the Master; that the Master asked him if all the rockets were white, and also asked him the time. (Gibson, 7553) Gibson stated that at this time the Master was awake. It was five minutes past

157

two, and Gibson returned to the bridge to Mr. Stone and reported. They both continued to keep the ship under observation until she disappeared. Mr. Stone describes this as "A gradual disappearing of all her lights, which would be perfectly natural with a ship steaming away from us."

At about 2.40 a.m. Mr. Stone again called up the Master by voice pipe and told him that the ship from which he had seen the rockets come had disappeared bearing SW. 1/2 W., (Stone, 7976) the last he had seen of the light; and the Master again asked him if he was certain there was no colour in the lights. "I again assured him they were all white, just white rockets." (7999) There is considerable discrepancy between the evidence of Mr. Stone and that of the Master. The latter states that he went to the voice pipe at about 1.15, but was told then of a white rocket (not five white rockets). (Lord, 6790) Moreover, between 1.30 and 4.30, when he was called by the chief officer (Mr. Stewart), he had no recollection of anything being reported to him at all, although he remembered Gibson opening and closing the chart room door. (6859)

Mr. Stewart relieved Mr. Stone at 4 a.m. (Stewart, 8571) The latter told him he had seen a ship four or five miles off when he went on deck at 12 o'clock, and 1 o'clock he had seen some white rockets, and that the moment the ship started firing them she started to steam away. (8582) Just at this time (about 4 a.m.) a steamer came into sight with two white masthead lights and a few lights amidships. He asked Mr. Stone whether he thought this was the steamer which had fired rockets, and Mr. Stone said he did not think it was. At 4.30 he called the Master and informed him that Mr. Stone had told him he had seen rockets in the middle watch. (8615) The Master said, "Yes, I know, he has been telling me." (8619) The Master came at once on to the bridge, and apparently took the fresh steamer for the one which had fired rockets, (8632) and said, "She looks all right; she is not making any signals now." This mistake was not corrected. He, however, had the wireless operator called.

At about 6 a.m. Captain Lord heard from the "Virginian" that the "'Titanic' had struck a berg, passengers in boats, ship sinking"; and he at once started through the field ice at full speed for the position given. (Lord, 7002)

Captain Lord stated that about 7.30 a.m. he passed the "Mount Temple," (7014) stopped, and that she was in the vicinity of the position given him as where the "Titanic" had collided (lat. 41° 46' N.; long. 50° 14' W.). (7026) He saw no wreckage there, but did later on near the "Carpathia," which ship he closed soon afterwards, and he stated that the position where he subsequently left this wreckage was 41° 33' N.; 50° 1' W. It is said in the evidence of Mr. Stewart that the position of the "Californian" was verified by stellar observations at 7.30 p.m. on the Sunday evening, and that he verified the Captain's position given when the ship stopped (42° 5' N.; 50° 7' W.) as accurate on the next day. The position in which the wreckage was said to have been seen on the Monday morning was verified by sights taken on that morning.

All the officers are stated to have taken sights, and Mr. Stewart in his evidence remarks that they all agreed. (Stewart, 8820) If it is admitted that these positions were correct, then it follows that the "Titanic's" position as given by that ship when making the C.Q.D. signal was approximately S. 16° W. (true), 19 miles from the "Californian"; and further that the position in which the "Californian" was stopped during the night, was thirty miles away from where the wreckage was seen by her in the morning, or that the wreckage had drifted 11 miles in a little more than five hours.

There are contradictions and inconsistencies in the story as told by the different witnesses. But the truth of the matter is plain. (7020) The "Titanic" collided with the berg 11.40. The vessel seen by the "Californian" stopped at this time. The rockets sent up from the "Titanic" were distress signals. The "Californian" saw distress signals. The number sent up by the "Titanic" was about eight. The "Californian" saw eight. The time over which the rockets from the "Titanic" were sent up was from about 12.45 to 1.45 o'clock. It was about this time that the "Californian" saw the rockets. At 2.40 Mr. Stone called to the Master that the ship from which he'd seen the rockets had disappeared.

At 2.20 a.m. the "Titanic" had foundered. It was suggested that the rockets seen by the "Californian" were from some other ship, not the "Titanic." But no other ship to fit this theory has ever been heard of.

These circumstances convince me that the ship seen by the "Californian" was the "Titanic," and if so, according to Captain Lord, the two vessels were about five miles apart at the time of the disaster. The evidence from the "Titanic" corroborates this estimate, but I am advised that the distance was probably greater, though not more than eight to ten miles. The ice by which the "Californian" was surrounded was loose ice extending for a distance of not more than two or three miles in the direction of the "Titanic." The night was clear and the sea was smooth. When she first saw the rockets the "Californian" could have pushed through the ice to the open water without any serious risk and so have come to the assistance of the "Titanic." Had she done so she might have saved many if not all of the lives that were lost.

21st Century Note: This is an excerpt from the official 1912 investigation by the British Board of Trade, but it is not the final word on the subject. Captain Lord did not have an opportunity to defend himself during the investigation, even though he had his own side of the story to tell. After the Titanic's wreck was found on the seabed in 1985, more credence could be given to a couple of the claims Captain Lord had made in 1912, namely, that the Titanic had not been as close to the Californian as previously thought, and that an unidentified ship may also have been in the vicinity that night, the lights of which may have been confused with the Titanic's.

III
Facts

I have garnered the facts in this section from many sources—books, websites, physical and online magazines, and television broadcasts. In most cases, I have verified the information by checking several sources, and then I have written a condensed summary statement. In the parentheses after each fact listed, there is a simple notation of what my primary source was. There may be small bits of data in my summary statement that I did not obtain from that primary source, but from the other sources that I checked. If the fact came primarily from a book, you can find more information in the bibliography at the end of this book. Otherwise, you can always find additional information by using search terms online.

Much has been lost in translation from the colorful, three-dimensional world to the old-fashioned medium of paper and ink. Much more exciting and interesting presentations of some of the facts can be found online, especially on YouTube. I will never forget the exquisite BBC video I saw of Weedy Seadragons dancing. The 114-character YouTube address for this video is too cumbersome. If you're interested, just do a search for "Weedy seadragons dance into the night." I myself have uploaded to YouTube beautiful multimedia presentations of Laura E. Richards' poem, "The Mermaidens" and Eugene Field's poem, "Wynken, Blynken, and Nod." You can find these at my YouTube site:

www.youtube.com/user/IdyllicProductions.

Discovering all these facts has been a great adventure for me. With the marvels of technology, including the internet, they were easily accessed. An ocean of information can be brought to us via undersea cables by a simple click.

Physical Features

The earth's longest mountain chain is underwater, extending approximately 50,000 miles through all the oceans. (*Britannica*)

Seventy-five percent of Earth's volcanoes are in its oceans. (National Oceanic and Atmospheric Administration)

"The Ring of Fire" is a series of trenches and volcanoes that extends for 25,000 miles along the Pacific Ocean floor. (National Oceanic and Atmospheric Administration)

Subduction zones, in which one of the earth's crustal plates slides under another, are responsible for massive earthquakes and tsunamis, such as the one which stuck Japan in 2011. A subduction zone lies in the sea about 150 miles west of Portland, Seattle, and Vancouver. Cliffs and valleys along this zone are twice the size of the Grand Canyon. Scientists did not realize the extent of this threat until they were doing research related to the Mt. St. Helens eruption in 1980. ("Drain the Oceans" broadcast, *National Geographic*)

Discovered in 1977, hydrothermal vents are the result of seawater descending through fissures in the ocean crust where two tectonic plates are moving away or toward each other. The cold seawater is heated by hot magma and reemerges to form the vents. They are found in all the oceans' basins, but they are most abundant around the Pacific's Ring of Fire. (National Oceanic and Atmospheric Administration)

"Black Smokers" are chimney-like structures that form (from deposits of iron sulfide) on the seafloor at hydrothermal vents and spew extremely hot, mineral-laden fluid. They can be as high as 65 feet, although this height does not usually last for long. "White Smokers" form from deposits of barium, calcium, and silicon, which are white. (*National Geographic*)

In the vicinity of hydrothermal vents, valuable mineral deposits can be found, including silver, gold, cobalt, nickel, and manganese. (*Smithsonian Ocean*)

New seafloor is constantly being created by molten rock which rises from below, as the earth's tectonic plates spread apart. (National Oceanic and Atmospheric Administration)

Because the tectonic plates are shifting, the Atlantic Ocean is growing slightly wider and the Pacific Ocean slightly smaller (one inch per year). (*101 Facts About Oceans*)

Islands are usually the tops of mountains or volcanoes that are connected to the seafloor. Greenland is the largest island on Earth. The Hawaiian Islands were built up from layers of lava. (SoftSchools)

On 11/14/63, the captain and cook of a trawler sailing south of Iceland saw smoke arising from the sea. Thinking that they might be looking at a fire on board a ship, they sailed closer to investigate. It was not a ship in trouble, though, but a new island being born. After a few days, the island had risen 147 feet above sea level, and eventually the lava flows formed a cap of solid rock, which prevented the waves from washing away the island. The island was named, "Surtsey." (Earthsky)

Even though parts of the Mariana Trench are the deepest spots on earth (deeper than Mt. Everest is high), other spots are closer to the earth's center— namely, oceanic points that are nearer to the North and South Poles. This is because the earth is not a perfect sphere. (Wikipedia)

The average depth of the ocean is 2.359 miles. "Challenger Deep," considered the deepest point, is 6.856 miles. The water pressure there is the equivalent of one person trying to support fifty jumbo jets. (Marinebio)

The Pacific Ocean is the world's largest, deepest ocean, and it contains approximately 25,000 islands. (350Pacific)

There are many thousands of islands in Indonesia (the exact number varies according to the source). Because of the 125 active volcanoes in the area and the rising ocean levels, the inhabitants of these islands are at continual risk of flooding and tsunamis. (CNN) Many small and low-lying islands are vulnerable to being permanently flooded. Jakarta, the capital of Indonesia, will probably be uninhabitable within twenty years. (WorldAtlas.com)

A tiny uninhabited island in northwest Hawaii, East Island, was obliterated by Hurricane Walaka on 10/3/18 and 10/4/18. The eleven-acre stretch of land had been an important nesting site for the threatened Hawaiian Green Sea Turtle and the Hawaiian Monk Seal. These animals had finished their breeding season and were no longer on the island when the hurricane struck, but it is unknown where they will go, when it's time for them to nest again. Sea Turtles generally return to the very beach where they were born, to lay their eggs. (Live Science)

The speed of sound in water is nearly five times faster than the speed of sound in air. (Marinebio)

In some places, there are rivers and lakes at the bottom of the ocean. These are formed by thick layers of salt which are sometimes present in the underlying bed. When the salt mixes with seawater, it becomes denser than the surrounding water, forming rivers or lakes, which can be very similar to lakes and rivers on land, with shorelines, surfaces, and even waves. (National Oceanic and Atmospheric Administration)

Lakes on the ocean floor can be over 300 feet deep. Scientists believe that some of these lakes host species that are specific to this environment. (worldatlas.com)

With warming water and air temperatures around the world, scientists are observing ice melting and moving from land-based sources on Antarctica and Greenland into the oceans. This combines with the water already in the oceans, raising the level of the entire sea surface. (Woods Hole Oceanographic Institution)

Antarctica is quite mountainous and has the highest average elevation of any continent. It also has at least one active volcano, Mount Erebus, and a sealed-off lake, Lake Vostok, which is the size of Lake Ontario. This lake lies two miles below the continental ice sheet and has been sealed off from air and light for millions of years. (Woods Hole Oceanographic Institution)

When Antarctic ice shelves freeze in the winter, the freezing water pushes out many salt particles, shoving them deeper into the ocean. This results in a massive underwater waterfall of cold, dense brine that cascades over the continental shelf and falls into an abyss about four and a half miles deep. The volume of this waterfall is equivalent to about 500,000,000 Niagara Falls. This brine helps regulate the temperature of all the world's oceans. (NV at CEP Imperial)

The Antarctic ice sheet vibrates constantly, humming at frequencies that are inaudible to humans, but almost audible to some whale species. Sped up, the sound resembles a didgeridoo-type instrument. (Live Science)

The world's tallest waterfall, other than the one off the Antarctic coast, is also underwater. It is in the Denmark Straight between Iceland and Greenland and is called the "Denmark Straight Sea Cataract." It is over two miles high, and the volume of water passing over it is equivalent to 2000 Niagara Falls. (Science.howstuffworks.com)

In recent history, the most powerful hurricane to hit New England's Cape Cod was Hurricane Bob in 1991, a Category Two storm. More powerful hurricanes have stricken New England in the past, however. Analysis of 30-foot-deep sediment cores shows that the area was hit by 23 hurricanes between 250 A.D. and 1150 A.D. that today would probably qualify as Category Three or Four. (Woods Hole Oceanographic Institution)

The highest tsunami ever recorded occurred on 7/9/58, when an earthquake produced a wave so tall that it removed millions of trees from locations as high as 1720 feet above sea level. The wave crashed against the southwest shoreline of Gilbert Inlet and continued down the length of Lituya Bay, into the Gulf of Alaska. (Geology.com)

According to researcher Molly Ranger, the asteroid that killed the dinosaurs created a tsunami 328 ft. high in the Gulf of Mexico and then moved through all the earth's oceans. It was thousands of times more powerful than the 2004 Indian Ocean tsunami. (Live Science)

Waves form deep in the oceans, as well as on the surface. The largest occur in the South China Sea, where they can grow to heights of 1640 feet. They do not usually cause damage on the surface. (Sciencealert.com)

The waters of the Atlantic churn relatively quickly because they interact with cold waters from both the North and South poles. The deep waters of the Pacific (below 1.5 miles) are more entrenched and have not seen the light of day for a thousand years. (Live Science)

At certain recognized points in the oceans, maelstroms or circular currents exist. They do not rise to the fictional threat level described by Edgar Allan Poe or Jules Verne, and they do not present much of a hazard to large ships, but they have been known to drown divers and create havoc for small ships. (Worldatlas.com)

A much more frightening hazard exists, which for centuries was thought to be fictional, but has now been shown to be real—rogue waves. They can appear out of nowhere and have been known to rise higher than 100 feet and roll even large ships over. Satellite images have confirmed their ongoing existence, and usually there are about ten rogue waves in the world's oceans at any given moment (defined as waves that are at least twice as high as the average high waves at that place and time). The unexplained 1918 disappearance of the USS Cyclops, with 309 men aboard, may have been due to a rogue wave, especially since the ship had a flat bottom which could roll easily. Efforts are currently being made to develop early warning systems and to improve the design of ships, so as to lessen the risks. (*National Geographic*, U.K.)

Some scientists theorize that rogue waves also played a role in the sinking of the SS Edmund Fitzgerald. At the time that this ship sank, another ship in the area, the SS Arthur M. Anderson, was hit by at least two 30-35 foot waves, which, according to the captain, continued on towards the Edmund Fitzgerald. (Engineering360)

According to the Australian National University, rogue wave holes (the inversion of rogue waves), also exist. In maritime folklore, stories of rogue holes are as common as stories of rogue waves, but their existence was not proven experimentally until 2012. (Australian National University)

The story of how ocean currents have been mapped is interesting. Two examples: Benjamin Franklin dropped bottles with messages in them into the Atlantic, asking finders to let him know where the bottles had been located. He used this data to chart ocean currents, including the Gulf Stream. (*How the World Works*) A plethora of toy rubber ducks have been sailing the seas since 1/10/92, when their shipping crate fell overboard in the Pacific, releasing 28,000 of them. Since then, some of the ducks have sailed separately to Alaska, Scotland, New England, Australia, and Indonesia, enabling researchers to study the currents that got them there. (*How the World Works*)

Legally, fifty percent of the United States lies beneath the ocean, according to explorer Robert Ballard, who discovered the Titanic thirty years ago. Because of the exclusive economic zone, which includes 200 nautical miles alongside the U.S. coast, there is as much sea bottom as there is dry land. (CBS News)

We generally think of sand as being beige, but on certain beaches in the following places and elsewhere, sand can be red, green, brown, purple, pink, white, orange, or black. For example, red and also green sand can be found on different beaches in Hawaii; brown and purple in California; pink in the Bahamas, Scotland, Puerto Rico, and the Philippines; white in Australia and Florida; orange in Portugal and Sardinia; black in Argentina, Tahiti, the Philippines, Hawaii, and Iceland. On Frazer Island in Australia, the sands are actually rainbow-colored, changing hue when the waves and winds shift and blow them. (Coastal Care)

Large amounts of sand are shipped to Singapore, the United Arab Emirates, and other small coastal countries, so that man-made islands can be built which extend the country's land mass. (*Discovery Magazine*)

For over 90% of human history, sea levels have been 130 feet – 425 feet lower than they are today. Thus the rising sea levels have destroyed much information about the lives of our ancestors. (The United Nations Educational, Scientific, and Cultural Organization)

The entire ocean floor has been mapped to some extent. All features on the seabed that are three miles or larger have been observed, at least via electronic equipment. The surfaces of Mars and Venus have been mapped to a much more detailed resolution. (worldatlas.com)

There are ancient and current sand dunes on Mars. Researchers have been measuring them in hopes of better understanding the planet's history. (*Discover Magazine*)

Explorations

While 70% of the earth's surface is covered by oceans, less than 5% of those oceans have been explored. (Woods Hole Oceanographic Institution)

Countless ancient buildings, settlements, cities, and port structures have been submerged over time. Some can now be found at active underwater archaeological sites. On the shores of the Mediterranean, 150 such cities and port structures have been located. (United Nations Educational, Scientific, and Cultural Organization)

In the Black Sea, there are remains of Mesolithic settlements dating back to 5000 B.C. (United Nations Educational, Scientific, and Cultural Organization)

In 2014 and 2015, Swiss and Greek archaeologists found a 4000 year old (Bronze Age) city submerged just a few feet beneath the surface of the Aegean Sea. The ruins stretch over twelve acres and many of the buildings are oval or circular in shape. A fortress was found, as well as paved surfaces that appear to have been streets. (History.com)

Off the coast of Norfolk, England, 4000 year old circular rings made of split oak trunks were found in 1998. (United Nations Educational, Scientific, and Cultural Organization)

Remains of prehistoric fish traps and clam gardens can be seen in a number of locations throughout the world, including South Africa, Denmark, Hawaii, Canada, and Australia. Some fish traps are complex arrangements of stone walls up to 1000 feet in length. (United Nations Educational, Scientific, and Cultural Organization)

In an undersea cave in France, the Cosquer Cave, there are paintings and engravings made between 27,000 and 19,000 years ago. The drawings are skillfully done and feature human hands and several animals, including horses, bison, deer, antelopes, seals, and fish, as well as abstract art. Although the entrance to the cave is now 121 feet underwater, the paintings described above are not submerged. (United Nations Educational, Scientific, and Cultural Organization)

In 22 B.C., King Herod created a seaport in Caesarea, Israel. The ruins have now been transformed into an underwater park for scuba divers. (United Nations Education, Scientific, and Cultural Organization)

There is a fleet of fourteen 5000-year-old ships beneath the sands of the Egyptian desert, six miles west of the Nile. It is thought that they were deliberately buried to serve the king in the afterlife. Sixty-feet long, they had space for thirty oarsmen. A brick case encloses each boat. In the same area, there is a structure seventy feet long and thirteen feet wide, with images of 120 different boats sketched into the interior walls. This structure probably originally housed a wooden funerary boat. (*National Geographic*)

1200 years after the Egyptians buried the fourteen ships mentioned above, they buried the legendary King Tutankhamun with 35 model boats instead of actual ships. (*National Geographic*)

The United Nations estimates that 3,000,000 sunken ships are scattered around ocean bottoms worldwide, many of them thousands of years old. When reached, these sites are almost like time capsules, providing first-hand information about life at the time of the sinking. (United Nations Educational, Scientific, and Cultural Organization)

Here are some common causes for centuries of shipwrecks: ship overloaded with cargo and/or poorly built, malfunctioning equipment, high seas, high winds, low visibility, encountering reefs or ice, unknowingly sailing into hurricanes or monsoons, fire, warfare, and piracy. (Shiprex.net)

According to Australian records, there were about 8000 wrecks around the continent over the past 400 years. Only 2000 have been located. (*Australian Geographic*)

Around 1000 shipwrecks lie off the Florida Keys, including that of the 360-foot-long Benwood. On a routine voyage in 1942, she collided with another vessel, the Robert C. Tuttle. The collision occurred because the two ships were completely blacked out, due to fears of German U-Boats in the area. (National Oceanic and Atmospheric Administration)

For over 200 years, people have been searching for pirate Jean Lafitte's caches of treasure in the vicinity of Barataria Bay, New Orleans. The Bay was home to a large fleet of pirates. In 1812, they were attacked by the U.S. Navy, and before fleeing, Lafitte supposedly buried several caches of gold and silver. Shortly after Hurricane Katrina struck the area in 2005, a man was tending to an uprooted oak tree in his yard, when he found a stash of gold and silver coins in the dirt. They were French and Spanish coins from the early 1800's. ("Mysteries at the Museum" broadcast, Travel Channel)

On 11/27/05, the ruins of a Spanish Galleon, sunk in 1708, were found at the bottom of the Caribbean Sea, 1968 feet below the surface. She housed a treasure of gold, silver, and emeralds, which is estimated to be worth somewhere between one and seventeen billion dollars today. Researchers from several countries were instrumental in the discovery, which used an underwater autonomous vehicle operated by the Woods Hole Oceano-graphic Institution, based in Massachusetts. As of early 2019, the treasure still remains on the seabed, due to legal battles about what should be done with it. (*Smithsonian Magazine*)

After a few limited expeditions to Antarctica in the late 1800's and early 1900's, many of which ended in disaster, the United States sent a full-scale expedition in 1947. It included 4700 men, 13 ships, and 23 airplanes. During this expedition, most of the coast was explored and photographed for mapping purposes. Today about forty countries operate research stations on Antarctica. (Swiss Polar Institute)

In addition to the subatomic particle research being done at the Large Hadron Collider in Switzerland, astrophysicists are also studying how neutrinos interact with atoms deep inside Antarctic ice. The continent is useful for this purpose because of its cold temperatures and remoteness. (*Scientific American*)

In the early 1960's, Jacques Cousteau did several experiments involving living in an undersea colony. In one, he and seven other people lived 33 feet down in the Red Sea in a starfish-shaped house for a month. As part of this experiment, two people lived in another structure 100 feet below the surface for a week, and Cousteau personally descended to 1000 feet, using a third vehicle that looked like a little yellow submarine. Perhaps there was no connection, but the Beatle's song, "Yellow Submarine" was first released in 1966. (*The Vintage News*)

Charles Lindbergh experienced hallucinations during his famous transatlantic flight. At times he buzzed the ocean's surface, so that the sea spray would keep him awake. He eventually became delirious from lack of rest, and he later wrote of seeing "vaguely outlined forms, transparent, moving, riding weightless with me in the plane," saying that the apparitions spoke with him and gave advice. (History.com)

In 1979, an American couple, Dorothy and John Peckham, were on a cruise to Hawaii when they wrote their names and post office box number on a note and slipped it into a bottle, along with a dollar bill. They threw the bottle overboard, and it was found three years later off Songkhla Beach in Thailand by Hoa Van Nguyen. At the time, Hoa Van Nguyen and his family were fleeing the communist regime in Vietnam. He spent the dollar on postage and contacted the Peckhams, who worked with U.S. Immigration to assist the family in obtaining refugee status and move to the United States. The Peckman's neighbors and the U.S. Catholic Welfare Bureau helped the Vietnamese family resettle. (*Los Angeles Times*)

In 1955, a Swedish sailor found his future wife by addressing his message in a bottle "To Someone Beautiful and Far Away." Two years later, when he returned home from another voyage, he found that a 17-year-old Sicilian woman had come across the bottle, had the message translated by a priest, and written back. Over time, letters, pictures, and marriage vows were exchanged. (*The American Weekly*)

Like the name suggests, "hovercrafts" ride on air, not on water. Because of this, they can progress over surfaces that would be problematic for regular boats. (Neoteric Hovercraft Inc.)

The Woods Hole Oceanographic Institute in Falmouth, Massachusetts (in the southwest corner of Cape Cod) employs "approximately 950 people, including more than 500 scientists, engineers, ship's crew, and technicians." It operates six research departments and more than 40 centers and labs. (Woods Hole Oceanographic Institute)

Sea Creatures

An estimated 50 – 80% of Earth's living species exist within the oceans. New marine life is continually being discovered. (MarineBio)

Over 70% of our planet's oxygen is produced in the ocean, mostly by marine plants, many of them microscopic. (*National Geographic*)

The Atlantic Sturgeon lives mainly in the open ocean, travelling independently, but it spawns in whatever freshwater river it was born in. When young, it generally remains in the river for several years before moving on to the sea. Individuals live for more than 60 years; the species has existed for more than 120,000,000 years, living simultaneously with dinosaurs. Once abundant, sturgeons are now an endangered species, due to historic overfishing, pollution, and damming of their spawning rivers. (Chesapeake Bay Foundation)

The Whale Shark, named "whale" for its size, is about the size of a school bus, and the largest fish in the sea (whales and squid are not fish). Considered a gentle giant, it feeds by swimming on the surface with its mouth open, catching plankton. Its coloration is striking, with stripes and polka dots. The average lifespan is 70 years. (*Britannica*)

Whales do not generally attack humans or ships, but there have been a couple of rare instances in which this happened. In 1820, an 85-foot sperm whale attacked the Essex, a large whaling ship, in the middle of the Pacific Ocean, causing her to sink. Her crew were left adrift in three small boats, and after more than 80 days at sea, only a few (out of 21) crew members survived. This real-life horror story reportedly inspired Herman Melville to write *Moby Dick*. The name for the fictional Moby Dick came from a real whale observed by sailors near the island of Mocha, near southern Chile. The sailors had named this whale, "Mocha Dick." Mocha Dick was albino, and according to legend, it had killed thirty men whose whaling efforts had previously left it with many injuries. (BBC News)

Fresh water sunfish are generally about ten inches long; ocean sunfish are eleven feet long. (*National Geographic*)

Another gentle giant, the Giant Japanese Spider Crab, resembles a spider with a leg span of up to

15 feet. It usually lives at least 500 feet down in the ocean, but it migrates up to 160 feet during breeding season. In order to blend in with its environment, it places sponges and other animals on top of its body. It lives for about 100 years. (The Tennessee Aquarium)

The largest Giant Squid recorded by scientists was almost 43 feet long. A frightening but elusive, blue-blooded creature, the Giant Squid can grab prey up to 33 feet away by shooting out its two feeding tentacles, which are tipped with hundreds of powerful suckers. Mariners used to think these squids were monsters and would attack boats, but no squid has been known to do so. (*Smithsonian*)

When fleeing predators such as sharks and tuna, some species of squid can actually fly away, briefly using their fins as wings to leap out of the water. (Vancouver Aquarium)

An amazing species of eel, ordinarily long and serpentine, can quickly inflate its head to the point where it looks like a black beach ball with a tail. The "ball" then splits and opens to create a huge mouth to use for prey. The tip of the tail of this "Deep Sea Pelican Eel" glows pink and occasionally flashes red. This eel is found in ocean depths of 500 to 6000 feet. (*Science Magazine*)

The octopus is a highly intelligent shape-shifter and escape artist. It can blend into its background, even an artificial background, almost completely by changing the color and texture of its skin. It has been known to turn red with anger and pale with fright, and it can recognize individual human faces. It can take on the appearance of other sea creatures such as crabs, snakes, or fish by collapsing and compressing most of its body. Because it is boneless, it can squeeze through very small spaces, and it knows exactly what size the space must be, in order for it to escape. If the hole is even slightly too small, the octopus knows in advance that it can't get out, and it doesn't make the effort. There have been instances in labs where octopuses leave their tank and open other tanks, feasting on fish or crabs, and then return to their own tank. (Natural History Museum) In 2016, at the New Zealand National Aquarium, an octopus slipped through a gap accidentally left at the top of his tank and then accessed and traversed a drain pipe down to the ocean. (*The Guardian*) In 2008, an octopus at the Sea Star Aquarium in Coburg, Germany, discovered he could extinguish the bright light shining into his aquarium by climbing onto the rim of his tank and squirting a jet of water at the light, thereby short-circuiting it. He continually did this until staff figured it out. This octopus also juggled crabs and threw rocks at the glass of his tank. (*The Telegraph*)

The largest known octopus species, the Giant Pacific Octopus, can reach sizes of more than 16 feet across. But it's generally only the small (5-8 inches) Blue-Ringed Octopus that is dangerous to humans. (*National Geographic*) This small octopus is not aggressive and would rather flee or show its blue rings as a warning, but it will sting if it is cornered. It carries enough venom to kill many humans in minutes, but victims often do not even know they have been stung until they become paralyzed and cannot breathe. (Ocean Conservancy)

Cuttlefish create amazing light shows to "hypnotize" prey. Also, like octopuses, they are very adept at transforming themselves to look like their environment, when they want to. Competition is fierce for females, and the smaller males of at least one species disguise themselves as females by changing their body color and even pretending to hold egg sacks. That way, the larger males unwittingly let them swim past and mate with the females. (Sciencentral)

One day, we might be wearing clothing that changes color, thanks to animals like the cuttlefish. Engineers at the University of Bristol are working on it. (British Broadcasting Corporation)

Cuttlefish ink used to be used as the dye called sepia, before artificial sepia was created. (*Britannica*)

Many deep-sea creatures, such as various species of fish, squid, krill, brittle stars, shrimp, and jellyfish, are bioluminescent. They usually glow with a bluish or greenish light, but some worms glow yellow, and at least one fish, the Stoplight Loosejaw, emits a red light, as well. (Natural History Museum, London)

Luminescent algae rescued Jim Lovell early in his career. As a 26-year-old naval pilot, he was undertaking a dangerous night-time training mission to protect an aircraft carrier under black-out conditions. When in mid-flight, his navigational panel short-circuited, and he lost track of his position. With the fuel running low, Jim lost radio contact and was now flying blind. He needed to make a precise landing on the carrier, with zero visibility and no instruments. He was able to do this only by following the path of luminescent algae which had been disturbed by the carrier's spinning propellers. Having successfully completed this training mission, he continued to accept challenging assignments and went on to become the spacecraft commander of Apollo 13 ("Mysteries at the Museum" broadcast, Travel Channel) Lovell was also the command module pilot of Apollo 8, the first Apollo mission to enter lunar orbit. (Wikipedia)

The Etmopterus lailae, a miniature shark that lives off the coast of Hawaii, is bioluminescent. (Scripps Institution of Oceanography)

Some jellyfish produce a glowing slime that can stick to a potential predator, thereby making it more vulnerable to its own predators. Some can also release their tentacles as glowing decoys. (Scripps Institution of Oceanography)

Travelers can go to many places in the world to witness bioluminescent beaches, including The Maldives, Bali, Puerto Rico, Jamaica, Hong Kong, Vietnam, Cambodia, and Japan. Sometimes bioluminescent beaches can be found in the United States, including along the east coast of Florida and Mission Bay in San Diego. The glow happens more frequently at some beaches than others. (Tripping.com)

Nudibranches, otherwise known as sea slugs, can be psychedelically colored, with bright purple, blue, and florescent orange. They steal toxins from their prey and use them for their own defense. (Natural History Museum, London)

The "Venus Flytrap Sea Anemone" is an animal that looks like a plant that feeds like an animal. All sea anemones are animals, but many look like colorful plants, some with fringed tops. (*Newsweek*)

Thought to be the true source of the "Unicorn" tusks that Vikings sold to gullible Europeans, Narwhals cannot be exhibited in aquariums, because they cannot survive the stress of captivity. The acidity and carbon dioxide levels in their blood decrease, and oxygen levels increase, when they are captured. If not returned to the ocean, they die. Left in their natural habitat, they usually live to the age of 100, their skin changing from blue/black to white as they age. (Weird Nature)

Blue Whales are considered the largest animal ever to have lived, including the dinosaurs. The whales grow to 98 feet, whereas, for example, the Diplodocus was only 85 feet. The blood vessels of the blue whale are large enough for a human to swim through. (British Broadcasting Corporation)

Whales produce some sounds that are inaudible to humans because they are below our frequency range. Basically, we cannot hear their bass notes, which can travel more than 10,000 miles at some ocean levels, or roughly, half way around the globe at the Washington D.C. latitudes. (Journey North) A scientific study of cortisol levels in whale earwax (from museum collections) has shown that whales were particularly stressed during the 1920's and 1930's, when the whaling industry was at its peak, and also during WWII, probably due to navel battles and underwater bombs. The study was led by researchers at Baylor University, Texas. (Natural History Museum, London)

The Giant Manta Ray can grow to be 23 feet across. Sadly, a 2200-pound Manta Ray was accidently caught by fishermen off the coast of Peru in 2015. (Earth Touch News Network)

After migrating thousands of miles through the ocean, sea turtles and salmon return to the same place that they themselves were born, in order to give birth. They use the earth's magnetic field. (ScienceDaily)

Banded Shrimp enter the jaws of sharks to clean their teeth. The sharks don't eat them. (*101 Facts about Oceans*)

Only two inches long, Pistol Shrimp provided cover for U.S. submarines during WWII by disrupting sonar tracking. The navy hid submarines in Pistol Shrimp beds because of the loud noises the shrimp produce. ("Mysteries at the Museum" broadcast, Travel Channel)

The male White-Spotted Pufferfish creates beautiful, seven-foot-wide circular designs on the sea floor off the Japan coast. In an effort to attract a mate, the little fish spends weeks building ornate, symmetrical patterns in the sand and decorating them with sand dollars and sea shells. In addition to the aesthetics, the pattern reduces the force of ocean currents in the center. ("Mysteries at the Museum" broadcast, Travel Channel)

One of the weirdest creatures in the sea is not a creature at all, but a colony of tiny creatures, called zooids, that link together to form a wide, partially transparent, luminescent, meandering tube, usually 26 to 60 feet long. Called a pyrosome, this tube feels like a soft feather boa. (*The Washington Post*)

Natural black pearls are especially prevalent around Tahiti and are formed in the Black Lip Oyster (Pinctada margaritifera). Cultured pearls come in many colors, partially due to the insertion of natural dyes. (Live Science)

Unlike the typical earthworm, sea worms take many interesting and colorful forms. One Acorn Worm, for example, resembles a purple iris. (Monterey Bay Aquarium Research Institute) Another looks like a green caterpillar with wild white and brown hair. (treehugger.com)

Before doing a true courtship dance, which can last up to eight hours, male and female seahorses establish a connection by intertwining their tails and swimming together every morning. Eventually, the female deposits her eggs somewhere in or on the male's body, usually in a pouch. (*National Geographic*)

There are at least 47 species of seahorses, ranging in size from half an inch to twelve inches. They have the ability to change their colors to blend in with the environment, so that various seahorses in various locations may appear yellow, red, purple, white, brown, or pink. Some also change colors as they dance with their partners. They are monogamous and some species mate for life. (*Smithsonian*)

The Leafy Seadragon, as a camouflage, grows extensions on its body that resemble seaweed. It can be found floating in clumps of seaweed, feeding on plankton and algae. It usually lives in the waters of southern and western Australia. (Sea and Sky)

A close cousin, the Weedy Seadragon, is polka dotted and striped, also with leafy extensions. It has been filmed doing an elaborate courtship dance, in which the male and female elegantly mirror each other's movements. (British Broadcasting Corporation)

The "Immortal Jellyfish" (Turritopsis dohrnii) can revert back to its juvenile state without dying, thereby starting its life all over again. It does this without a brain. Humans, who have brains, cannot figure out how the creature accomplishes this. (*National Geographic*)

The Lion's Mane Jellyfish is 120 feet long. It lives primarily in Arctic waters. (*National Geographic*)

Moon jellies, known for their round domes, change color depending upon what they eat. (*National Geographic*)

Jellyfish are not fish. They are a disparate group of animals that have a common characteristic—their bodies are gelatinous. (*National Geographic*)

Some species of sea cucumbers look more like broccoli—blue and orange broccoli, especially when their branch-like tentacles spread out. (Live Science)

Swordfish and Marlin are the fastest fish, briefly reaching speeds of 75 miles per hour. Bluefin Tuna can reach sustained speeds of 56 miles per hour. (marinebio.org)

Oarfish can grow up to 50 feet. Long and slim, they have silvery blue skin, blue gills, and a red dorsal fin which runs along the length of the back. (Sea and Sky)

The Dragon Fish has bright green or silver teeth that look fierce and glow in the dark. Some species can also produce a red light and project it like a spotlight ahead. (National Environmental Science Programme)

Sea otters whack clams, crabs, and other shellfish against large rocks to crack them. Later, when they sleep, they often wrap themselves in kelp, so they don't drift away in the ocean. (Oregon Coast Aquarium)

Most whales eat krill and small fish, but killer whales also eat seals, sea birds, great white sharks, and other whale species. (National History Museum, London)

The Bottlenose Dolphin can sleep while swimming, by shutting down half of its brain for two hours at a time, and then reversing and shutting down the other half. It usually pairs up with another dolphin to do this. (*Scientific American*)

When large whales die, their bodies provide life support for hundreds of marine animals for decades. (National Ocean Service)

In 2018, a new device was developed whereby marine biologists can collect, study, and release fragile invertebrates without harming the animals. The instrument looks like a robotic plastic flower and is origami-inspired. It was developed jointly by researchers from three institutions—Harvard University's Wyss Institute, John A. Paulson School of Engineering and Applied Science, and Radcliffe Institute for Advanced Studies. (*Discover Magazine*)

Researchers studying the DNA of giant tortoises have found that they possess a number of gene variants linked to DNA repair, immune response, and cancer suppression. This is opening up new lines for research on human aging. (Science Daily)

There are 500 to 700 species of cone snails, many with beautiful, cone-shaped shells, and each producing its own unique set of complex toxins, some dangerous to humans. In fact, some can produce different toxins to use on different prey as the snails mature. The good news is that the venom of Conus magus, or Magician's Cone Snail, has been studied and one of the peptides has been used to produce a powerful painkiller, Ziconotide. This painkiller is 1000 times more powerful than morphine, and prolonged use does not result in tolerance or addiction. It works by blocking calcium channels in pain-transmitting nerve cells, thereby stopping them from transmitting pain signals to the brain. It is being used to treat AIDS, cancer, and neurological disorders. Once such a peptide is discovered and analyzed, it can be manufactured artificially. (Carnegie Museum of Natural History) Ziconotide was the first drug to be derived from a marine species, and since it has been so success-ful, there is now a wave of new explorations into finding other sea organisms that can offer medical benefits. There are seemingly endless possibilities here, especially since so much marine life has yet to be discovered and/or studied. (University of Wisconsin)

Chemicals compounds from coral reef plants and animals have yielded treatments for cancer, heart disease, inflammation, and viral infections. In addition, because the structure and chemistry of coral is similar to human bone, it has been used to facilitate bone-grafting. (Coral.org)

The molecules that sponges make for defending themselves against bacteria may be useful for humans, as well. The first anti-leukemia drug was developed from two chemicals found in one sponge species. (Natural History Museum, London) Some of Antarctica's marine animals have unique chemical defenses that are being investigated as potential sources of antibiotics. (Nova)

Grains of sand may be inanimate, but whole communities of various microbes are living on them, per researchers at the Planck Institute for Marine Microbiology. (*Discover Magazine*)

There is a "dead zone" in the Arabian Sea which has now grown to about the size of Florida. Fish and other marine creatures cannot survive in this zone because massive algae growth uses all the oxygen in the water. The algae growth is fueled by nutrient-dense fertilizers and sewage. Warmer ocean temperatures may also play a role, since

warm water is less effective at retaining oxygen.
(Live Science)

According to research presented on 12/11/18 at the
American Geophysical Union meeting in Washington D.C., a colony of 1,500,000 penguins has been
newly discovered. Tests show that these birds have
remained hidden on their tiny Antarctic archipelago,
the Danger Islands, for at least 2800 years. Scientists had thought they knew where all the penguin
colonies were, until NASA automated the penguin
detection process. The automation led to this discovery. (Live Science)

Mysteries and Legends

Near the village of Callanish in the Outer Hebrides, Scotland, there are some impressive stone arrangements that predate Stonehenge by 2000 years. One is made up of monoliths between three and sixteen feet high, arranged in a cross-shaped pattern with a central stone circle of 13 stones. Nearby, there are at least two other circular formations, as well as other Neolithic structures. The original meaning and purpose of these constructions is a mystery, although perhaps they were used in rituals related to the moon and stars. (Calanais Visitor Center)

A highly accurate and complex astronomical calendar that has a maze of 30 interlocking gears was found in 1900, in the sunken wreckage of a Greek cargo ship that is at least 2000 years old. Called the Antikythera Mechanism, for years its function was a mystery. It is now known that this ingenious device can calculate the positions of Mars, Jupiter, Saturn, Mercury, Venus, and our sun and moon for any chosen date. (Live Science)

Historical instruments called astrolabes were used to inform seafarers of the current and upcoming positions of the sun, moon, and stars. Several astrolabes have been found in shipwrecks. (The United Nations Educational, Scientific, and Cultural Organization)

The 2nd century Greek mathematician, astronomer, and geographer, Ptolemy, claimed that certain islands were hazardous because of the large amount of lodestone on them. Per Ptolemy, any ship that had been constructed with iron nails would be drawn to the magnetic island, and it could never get away. (*The Asiatic Journal and Monthly Register for British and Foreign India, China, and Australia*)

Plato's account of the destruction of Atlantis can be partially supported by geological evidence between the ancient Pillars of Heracles. Between those pillars was situated a subduction zone that could have caused a series of fatal quakes and tsunamis. No evidence of substantial human structures has been found there. However, the possibility cannot be ruled out, because sea levels rose by 400 feet at the end of the last ice age, removing any evidence of the lives of early people living in the area. ("Drain the Oceans" broadcast, *National Geographic*)

The Book of John Mandeville, a 14th century work which purported to describe the amazing creatures, sights, and customs that the writer had observed during his extensive years of travel throughout the medieval world, was so popular that it was translated into eight languages. In the 19th century, it became clear that most of the things the author claimed to have seen were actually witnessed by him on the pages of his vast library, and not in the outside world. Today, scholars do not think the book was written by anyone named John Mandeville. In fact, such a person may never have existed. One of the things the author claimed to have witnessed were gold-infused mountains on the island of "Taprobane." He wrote that ferocious, dog-sized ants lived on the mountains and that they mined and refined the gold. If someone wanted to obtain some of that gold, he should wait until the ants went underground in the late morning to avoid the hot temperatures, and then go up the mountains with his camels and/or horses and load up as many sacks of gold as he could. (University of Rochester)

For many centuries, sailors thought that if they sailed beyond certain recognizable points, such as the western end of the Mediterranean, they risked falling off the edge of the world into a great abyss. Also, they believed that if they sailed too far out, they might get fatally close to the sun. (*Seafaring Lore & Legend*)

One had to treat cats well on board a ship, because not only could they predict the future, but they might create it, as evidenced by the lightning bolts in their tails (static electricity). (*Seafaring Lore & Legend*)

In his book, *Seafaring Lore & Legend*, Peter D. Jeans lists many superstitions that seafarers believed in. Since being out on the ocean was a risky venture, superstitions (however silly they may appear to us today) helped create an illusion of personal control in the face of the unknown. Here are a few examples:

A ship's name should not include any word which refers to fire, lightning, or storm, lest the chances of such a threat be increased.

Bare-breasted feminine figureheads were an asset, as they could help calm threatening seas.

Eyes should be painted on both sides of the bow to help the vessel navigate safely.

One should never whistle on board a ship, lest the god of the wind think he was being mocked and retaliate.

Waterspouts can damage ships and have terrified mariners. If the waterspout is a rare one that rotates clockwise in the Northern Hemisphere or counterclockwise in the Southern Hemisphere, it appears to coil around itself in a serpentine manner. Early sailors would therefore discharge artillery at it, in an effort to destroy it. (*Superstitions of the Sea*)

It was generally considered unlucky to have women aboard a ship, but many wives went to sea with their husbands, sometimes on voyages that lasted as long as five years. They did domestic chores, read, wrote, and gave birth to children, whom they tutored. (*Superstitions of the Sea*)

The Grateful Dead played a traditional sea ballad on their "Reckoning" album and sometimes in concert. Entitled "Jack-A-Roe," it tells the story of a woman from London who loved a sailor named Jack, who went to war in Germany. She dressed like a man and went on a voyage to the battleground. She then found Jack injured, carried him to town, and sent for a doctor. He recovered and they got married. (*The Complete Grateful Dead Songbook*)

In 1692, the astronomer Edmund Halley, who calculated the return of the comet, proposed that the earth was composed of four concentric spheres. This was the only way he could account for variances in the earth's magnetic field. Others added to the theory. Leonhard Euler, a Swiss mathematician, thought the earth was hollow and contained a 600-mile-wide sun that made it possible for an advanced civilization to live under-ground. American John Symmes, a former army officer and business man, believed there were entrances to this inner world at the north and south poles. He could not obtain funding for an expedition to prove it, but one of his followers helped influence the U.S. government to send an expedition to Antarctica in 1838. The team did not find any entrance to an inner world, but they did find evidence that Antarctica is actually a continent and not just an ice cap. Due to increasingly sophisticated technology, the hollow earth theory was eventually disproven in the late 18th century. (Museum of Unnatural History)

People in the early 1800's thought that when a ship sank, it never reached the ocean bottom, but instead the ship and its inhabitants floated ghostlike in dense water that nothing could sink through. (*Mapping the Deep*)

Until undersea telegraph cables started becoming encrusted with starfish and worms (in the 1860's), people thought that no animals could survive in the deep sea, because of water pressure, severe cold, and an absence of light. (*Mapping the Deep*)

In the early 1800's, a French naturalist sailed around the world measuring the temperature of the oceans. He found that the deeper he looked, the colder the water was, so he concluded that the seafloor was covered with a thick layer of ice. He overlooked the fact that ice floats. (*Mapping the Deep*)

On 1/23/1960, Jacques Piccard and Don Walsh descended into the deepest chasm on earth, the Mariana Trench, in a "bathyscaphe" (the Trieste). In the depths, they saw a flatfish resembling a sole. That erased all doubts that life could exist in the deep sea. (*Mapping the Deep*)

Ghost ships have allegedly been seen in many places worldwide. At least some of them can be explained as mirages or sound distortions due to atmospheric conditions, especially when a storm is nearby. Eyestrain, fatigue, and stress may also contribute. (*Folklore and the Sea*)

Fata Morgana is a type of mirage that appears during ocean voyages or on the Great Lakes. It makes distant objects such as ships or islands appear to be floating in the air on the horizon, sometimes upside down. The changeable image can be very complex and unusual, involving several inverted and/or erect images layered on top of one another, so that it looks like an enchanted landscape or city. It is caused by light's being refracted by contrasting air temperatures. The name comes from the sorceress in the legend of King Arthur, Morgan le Fay. (Mother Nature Network)

In the early 1900's, Artic explorer Donald MacMillan was attempting to find an alleged island, "Crocker Island," which Robert Peary claimed to have seen at a distance about six years earlier. After having had an extremely difficult time getting to the frozen location, MacMillan insisted that he and his remaining three companions continue the search for five more days, despite the opinion of at least one of his Inuit companions that what they had seen was not an island at all, but a mirage. After five fruitless days, MacMillan had to admit that his companion was right—it was probably an instance of Fata Morgana. In 1938 a plane flew over the area and confirmed that "Crocker Island" did not exist. (*Natural History Magazine*)

One of the most famous sea mysteries involves the Mary Celeste, which set sail from New York Harbor on 11/7/1872 with ten people on board, including an experienced captain and his two-year-old daughter. On 12/5/1872, a passing British ship found the Mary Celeste drifting off the Azores essentially undamaged, with a missing lifeboat, and no individuals on board. Many theories have emerged over the years as to what happened to the inhabitants, none conclusive. Several other misfortunes befell that same ship (formerly named "Amazon"), before and after the above events. (Smithsonian)

The Zebrina was a barge that ran aground in France in 1917. When it was found, the crew of five were missing, and they have never been found. (Live Science)

The Flying Dutchman is a legendary ghost ship and a portent of doom. The myth probably has its origins in the 1600's, during the heyday of the Dutch East India Company. Allegedly, there was a Captain Hendrick van der Decken, who was blasphemously obstinate and would not heed the warnings of his crew or the weather. As a result, his ship sank in 1641, being cursed and doomed to sail the oceans forever as a ghost ship, bringing bad fortune to all who see it. There have been alleged sightings of the ship as late as the 19th and 20th centuries. (Wikipedia)

In Disneyland's Haunted Mansion, there is an activated painting of The Flying Dutchman as it encounters a thunderstorm and the sails become ravaged. (Wikipedia)

Another legend about an unfortunate ship involves the Octavius, which set sail in China in 1761, bound for London. The captain, rather than sailing established routes, decided to try to find a way to London through the Artic, where the ship became trapped in ice. Everyone on board died when the food and fuel ran out, but when the sea ice thawed the following summer, the ship drifted on its own through the (as yet undiscovered) Northwest Passage. The ship was found off the coast of Greenland by the whaling ship, the Herald, in 1775, 13 years later. The captain and several crew members investigated the drifting ship and found 27 bodies frozen in place, looking like they had just died. The last entry in the Octavius' log had been made on 11/11/1762. It is unknown if this ship actually existed, but other ships and men were lost in early efforts to find the Northwest Passage.

On 8/6/1848, the HMS Daedalus reportedly had a 20-minute encounter with a sea serpent 300 miles off the southern coast of Africa. The captain and two other witnesses provided highly detailed and convincing accounts of the "serpent," including a sketch of what they had seen. This created quite a stir in London, and an eminent scientist at the time suggested that the creature might have been a large elephant seal. The captain denied this and went to his grave saying he had seen a sea monster. In 2015, evolutionary biologist Dr. Gary Galbreath reviewed the diary, notes, and sketch, and suggested that the creature was a Sei baleen whale, which would probably have been unknown to the captain and crew of the Daedalus. These little-known whales are 55 feet long and swim on their sides with their dorsal fin in the air as they feed on the surface. According to Dr. Galbreath, this would resemble the creature in the sketch. ("Mysteries at the Museum" broadcast, Travel Channel)

For centuries, there have been other reports of Sea Serpents. In 1779, a naval officer claimed that he saw a serpentine creature with a long neck off the coast of Maine. Many other sightings of this creature, dubbed "Cassie," have been reported since then. One of the more logical explanations for these sightings is that this is a sperm whale—a 50-foot whale that, when breeding, flips over on its back and swims with its four-foot penis up in the air (thus the long "neck"). ("Mysteries at the Museum" broadcast, Travel Channel)

From 1638 to 1962, there were reports of a sea serpent off the coast of Gloucester, Massachusetts. Hundreds of people claimed to have seen it. (*The Appendix*)

On 8/11/1937, 60-inch webbed footprints were discovered on the island of Nantucket, Massachusetts. Shortly thereafter, locals started seeing a huge green creature with big bulbous eyes moving in the waves. Naturally this created quite a stir, with the public hanging on every word from the press. The mystery was resolved a few days later, when a huge rubber balloon in the shape of a sea monster was found resting on the beach. It had been created by Tony Sarg, the noted puppeteer and theatrical designer who introduced the enormous inflatable cartoons and caricatures to the Macy's Thanksgiving Day Parade. That's where the sea monster went next. The local newspaper was in on the gag. ("Mysteries at the Museum" broadcast, Travel Channel)

In 1970, a decomposing body of a 30-foot sea creature washed up on the beach in Scituate, MA. It did not look like anything the local population was familiar with, and the press dubbed the animal "Cecil, the Sea-Sick Sea Serpent." An expert from the New England Aquarium identified it as a Basking Shark. ("Mysteries at the Museum" broadcast, Travel Channel)

Mariners used to believe that cats were endowed with ESP and were therefore able to foretell disasters. On 11/26/1898, (before the age of hurricane forecasting) the "Portland" was getting ready to depart from Boston, when several would-be passengers saw the ship's cat carry her litter of kittens off the vessel and into a nearby warehouse. Those who saw this omen did not embark on the voyage. This saved their lives, because the ship sank in a hurricane that night. A similar incident occurred in 1955 on the Joyita, a ship out of Apia, Samoa. The ship's cook was especially fond of the ship's cat, but one day the cat seemed to be in extreme agitation, and when he tried to calm her, she scratched him and ran off the ship. The vessel departed, but never reached her destination. It was found two months later, and despite an exhaustive search, no trace was ever found of the crew or passengers. (*Superstitions of the Sea*)

Some of the shipwrecks that have occurred in the Bermuda Triangle may be attributed to topography. Bermuda is a flattened volcanic mountaintop, with treacherous reefs that have built up from its slopes. On the reefs are limestone structures that are harder than the surrounding reef, have sharp points, and can break the surface at low tide. They can pierce a ship's hull, especially when they are just under the surface and less visible in calm seas. ("Drain the Oceans" broadcast, *National Geographic*)

The concept of the mermaid is fairly universal worldwide and goes back at least six thousand years. The first merman in recorded history is the fish-tailed Babylonian god Ea, who was sometimes depicted as human to the waist. The first mermaid was Atargatis, a Semitic moon goddess. (*Sea Enchantress*)

There have been many detailed accounts of firsthand, closeup encounters with mermaids and mermen, even as recently as the 19th century.

Some of these reports were not given by fringe elements in society, but by well-respected leaders. Some instances were described by multiple witnesses. For example, in 1830, inhabitants of Benbecula, Scotland, stated that they had seen a little mermaid playing happily in the surf. Several men walked out into the water to capture her, but she swam beyond their grasp. A little boy threw stones at her, one of which struck her in the back. Several days later, her body was washed to shore. Upon examination she was found to be about the size of a three or four-year-old, but with an abnormally developed breast and a lower body like that of a salmon. Her hair was long, dark, and glossy, and her skin was white. Crowds came to see her, a coffin and shroud were made for her, and she was buried near the shore where she was found. (*Sea Enchantress*)

On 10/31/1881, a Boston newspaper published the following account of a mermaid captured in Aspinwall Bay: "This wonder of the deep is in a fine state of preservation. The head and body of a woman are very plainly and distinctly marked. The features of the face, eyes, nose, mouth, teeth, arms, breasts, and hair are those of a human being. The hair on its head is of a pale, silky blonde, several inches in length. The arms terminate in claws closely resembling an eagle's talons instead of

fingers with nails. From the waist up, the resem-
blance to a woman is perfect, and from the waist
down, the body is exactly the same as the ordinary
mullet of our waters, with its scales, fins and tail
perfect. Many old fishermen and amateur anglers
who have seen it pronounce it unlike any fish they
have ever seen. Scientists and savants alike are 'all
at sea' respecting it, and say that if the mermaid be
indeed a fabulous creature, they cannot class this
strange comer from the blue waters." (*Sea
Enchantress*, taken from F.S. Bassett's *Legends
and Superstitions of Sailors and the Sea*, 1885)

Medieval Christian churches adopted the popular
belief in mermaids, in part as a vehicle for warning
men against the treachery of feminine charms. The
mermaid was seen as a character who could not be
trusted and who could destroy ships or otherwise
lure men to their deaths. In their 1961 book, *Sea
Enchantress; The Tale of the Mermaid and her Kin*,
Gwen Benwell and Authur Waugh list 45 examples
of mermaid images having been incorporated into
the designs of British cathedrals and churches,
including Westminster Abbey. In two of these
(Norwich Cathedral and Wells Cathedral in Somer-
set), she is portrayed as suckling a lion. (*Sea
Enchantress*)

Some alleged mermaid sightings may actually have been seals. Seals sit on rocks at the seashore, have some humanoid gestures and expressions, a round head, and sometimes follow boats for their own purposes, like fishing. (*Sea Enchantress*)

Western Celts and Scandinavians believed mermaids were fallen angels, or human beings that had had a spell cast upon them, or the souls of men drowned at sea. (*Sea Enchantress*)

From the 16th through the 19th centuries, fake mermaids were created, usually from the upper half of a monkey and the tail of a fish, and were exhibited for the public, along with stories about how these "mermaids" were discovered and captured. At one point, the skill involved in producing these monstrosities was even considered an art form. (*Sea Enchantress*)

Mermaids and mermen were not the only legendary humanoid sea creatures. There were also the "seal people" or "selkies," who were seals at sea and humans on land. According to historian John MacAulay, the alleged selkies were probably people coming down from the north whose clothes and kayaks were made of sealskin. (*Secrets of the Sea House*)

In 2010, during the rebuilding process at the World Trade Center site, construction workers unearthed a mystery—a 32-foot-long ship buried in the rubble, 22 feet below today's street level. Research was done on the make and model of the ship, using the pattern of natural rings in the wood. The ship was traced to a small shipyard near Philadelphia, which probably built it in 1773. As to how it ended up in the vicinity of the Twin Towers, it was probably being used as landfill, when Manhattan was expanded by 1000 feet on each side in the early 1800's. Much of today's financial district was underwater at the time, and large quantities of wood from various sources were dumped into the water to create more land. (*Huffington Post*)

Submarines

Leonardo da Vinci drew a rough sketch of a sub-marine in 1500. A primitive submarine called the "Turtle" was ineffectively used during the American Revolution. The first successful use of a submarine was during the American Civil War. (*The Sea and Civilization; A Maritime History of the World*)

The ocean liner Lusitania was struck by a German torpedo on her 1915 journey from New York to Liverpool, after its captain had ignored warnings by the German Embassy and the British Admiralty. (History.com) During the 18 or so minutes that it took the ship to sink, at least one passenger wrote a message and put it in a bottle: "Still on deck with a few people. The last boats have left. We are sinking fast. Some men near me are praying with a priest. The end is near. Maybe this note will . . ." (note unfinished) (Posted by Melissa Brayer to Mother Nature Network)

In 1921, a U.S. submarine (USS R14) ran out of fuel about 100 nautical miles from Hawaii. The radio also malfunctioned, and the crew was low on food. They managed to rescue themselves by turning the heavy steel sub into a sailing ship.

Bedsheets, hammocks, towels and mattress covers were stitched together and stretched between frames made from metal beds. Then these make-shift sails were attached to high points on the sub. Sailing at four miles an hour, and rationing their food, they made it to a harbor in Hawaii in about three days. ("Mysteries at the Museum" broadcast, Travel Channel)

The Queen Mary's 2332 passengers had a harrow-ing ride when they left Great Britain on 8/30/1939. Many had curtailed their vacations so that they would not be trapped on the wrong side of the Atlantic when war broke out. Just a few hours after Britain's ultimatum was delivered to Germany, the Queen Mary's captain received an urgent dispatch to sail about 100 miles south of her normal route as a precaution against German submarines and to "take all necessary precautions." The crew painted over portholes and rigged blackout curtains on doorways. Extra lookouts watched for periscopes. The captain asked passenger Bob Hope to do a show, which he did, to lighten the mood. Two days into the voyage, the German army invaded Poland. The Queen Mary was left unmolested. She arrived safely in New York City on 9/5/1939. Then she was put into military service, and she aided the war effort by transporting troops and Italian and Ger-man POW's. (Warfare History Network)

A typo greatly aided the war effort, too. In 1939, the U.S. military mistakenly hired a Cryptogamist (an expert in seaweed, fungi, and algae), instead of a Cryptogramist (an expert in codebreaking). They transported Geoffrey Tandy, the marine biologist, to Bletchley Park, a secret military installation, and informed him that his job was to help crack the infamous German Enigma Code. The mistake soon came to light, but at that point, the scientist knew too much, and he was not allowed to return home. As fate would have it, though, his services came in very handy a couple of years later, when the British navy torpedoed a German submarine and recovered a waterlogged codebook for the German Enigma machine. The book was brought to Bletchley Park, but codebreakers could not handle it or work with it, because it was disintegrating. Tandy covered the waterlogged pages with specialized absorbent sheets that he usually used to dry off delicate sea specimens. Within a few hours, the sheets could be handled, and working day and night, the codebreakers were able to break the code within a few months. This enabled the U.S. navy to pinpoint the locations of German submarines across the Atlantic. ("Mysteries at the Museum" broadcast, Travel Channel)

Along the U.S. East Coast, there are hundreds of wrecks sunk by German submarines. American merchant ships were sunk as they tried to carry vital supplies like oil, gasoline, food, lumber, and rubber to allies in Europe. Cape Hatteras was especially besieged because of its topography, and because the officials were slow to order blackouts. Off the Hatteras shore, the sea bottom drops off quickly, which enabled the subs to easily move out to deeper water for extra cover. To prevent panic, the authorities initially banned news of attacks on America's shores and failed to order blackouts in a timely manner. Therefore, at night, the Germans had a clear view of the ships. In 1942, the U.S. mobilized coastal air patrols and issued blackout orders. Americans were ordered to extinguish all street lights on waterfront streets, to screen all advertising lights and lighted windows facing seaward, and to dim automobile headlights along the coast. ("Drain the Oceans" broadcast, *National Geographic*)

Miscellaneous

When theatrical staging became more sophisticated during the Renaissance, sailors were hired to set up and manage the curtains. This was because they were familiar with rigging sails and raising, lowering, twisting, and tying ropes on ships. The stage was called "the deck." (Ocean Treks with Jeff Corwin broadcast)

The creation of the transatlantic steamship in the early 1800's shortened transatlantic travel time from three weeks eastbound, and twelve weeks westbound, to less than two weeks either way. By the end of the century, it was down to six days. (*The Sea and Civilization; A Maritime History of the World*)

In the 19th century, due to the booming whaling industry, New Bedford, Massachusetts was the richest city per capita in the world. A terrible price was paid, however, as evidenced by all the memorial tablets displayed in the Seamen's Bethel. These tablets commemorate the lives and deaths of whalers and fisherman who perished in this brutal and dangerous business. (National Park Service)

The Harvard University Museum of Comparative Zoology in Cambridge, Massachusetts houses an exquisite collection of glass invertebrates created by the same father-and-son team that created Harvard's glass flower collection. The zoology collection includes approximately 430 models of beautiful and anatomically correct marine and terrestrial invertebrates, including sea anemones, squid, jellyfish, octopus, sea cucumber, and marine worms. These glass creatures were created in the 1870's and 1880's by Leopold and Rudolf Blaschka in their studio in Dresden, Germany. In May of 2014, a permanent exhibition of the Blaschka's zoological work was opened at the adjacent Harvard Museum of Natural History. It consists of a rotating selection of approximately 60 models. (Harvard University)

Between 1886 and 1902, the Statue of Liberty was used as a lighthouse. About a month after the statue was dedicated on 10/28/86, it became operational as a lighthouse. The torch in Lady Liberty's right hand contained nine electric arc lamps that could be seen 24 miles out to sea. Electric light was a fairly new invention at the time, and the station's keeper was chosen because he had specialized knowledge of electricity. On 3/1/1902, the lighthouse was discontinued as an aid to navigation. (lighthousefriends.com)

Although the Titanic had received at least five messages from five other ships over the course of the fateful day, warning of treacherous ice in the area, the ship continued to travel at the same high speed that it had been going—about 22 knots, according to the British government report. This was the general practice of ocean liners at the time—to keep a fast pace, while trusting a sharp lookout to keep the vessel out of danger. (The Loss of the Titanic—official government report)

Several days after the Titanic disaster, her sister ship the Olympic was loading at Southampton, England, preparing for a transatlantic trip, when the entire crew of firemen and trimmers walked off the ship and refused to return until a sufficient number of seaworthy lifeboats were put on board to accommodate every passenger and crew member. This led to a number of confrontations with the White Star Management, and 54 sailors were eventually charged with mutiny. Fearing public retribution, though, the White Star management backed down, and the court imposed no penalty on the strikers. (Wikipedia)

Biologist Charles Anderson has studied the migration patterns of Globe Skimmer Dragonflies (Pantala flavescens) He believes they make use of moving weather systems and monsoon rains to complete an epic migration from southern India to Africa, and then likely back again, a round trip of 10,000 miles over open ocean. A single dragonfly does not do it—it takes four generations to make the full round trip each year. (BBC)

90% of international trade travels by ship. (Woods Hole Oceanographic Institute)

98% of the internet runs via undersea fiber optic cables, at 99.7% the speed of light. In the deepest parts of the ocean, the cable is laid directly on the sea floor, but in most places, it is buried 10-12 feet deep below the seabed, in trenches made by plows the size of houses. ("Drain the Oceans" broadcast, National Geographic)

The remains of about 200 ships from the Revolutionary War, the Civil War, World War I, and World War II were deliberately deposited in Mallows Bay, Maryland, a part of the Potomac River. Some of these shipwrecks have moved over time, due to storms, floods, and erosions. (Live Science)

Since 1971, hundreds of crash-landing spacecraft and associated debris, including the Russian MIR space station, have been intentionally guided to Point Nemo. This is a remote spot in the middle of the South Pacific Ocean, named for Jules Verne's Captain Nemo. The debris lies 2.5 miles below the ocean's surface. (Live Science)

Over the last two decades, cargo ships have tripled in size. Now the largest ships are almost as long as four football fields and as tall as 20-story buildings. This has necessitated expensive changes to the Panama Canal and to any commercial harbors that want to stay in the business. ("Mega Machines: Sea Giants" broadcast, Science Channel)

Bibliography

Barnes, Julia. *101 Facts About Oceans*. Milwaukee, WI: Gareth Stevens Publishing, 2004

Beck, Horace. *Folklore and the Sea*. Edison, N.J.: Castle Books, 1999

Benwell, Gwen and Waugh, Arthur. *Sea Enchantress; The Tale of the Mermaid and her Kin*. New York, N.Y.: The Citadel Press, 1965

Campbell, William Wilfred. *Selected Poetry and Essays*. Ontario, Canada: Wilfrid Laurier University Press, 1987.

Carman, Bliss. *The World's Best Poetry*. Great Neck, N.Y.: Granger Book Company, Inc., 1981

Carman, Bliss and Hovey, Richard. *Last Songs from Vagabondia*. Boston, MA: Forgotten Books, 2012. Originally Published 1900.

Clary, James. *Superstitions of the Sea*. St. Clair, MI: Maritime History in Art, 1994.

Dorian, Christiane. *How the World Works*. Surrey, U.K.: Templar Publishing, 2010.

Doyle, Arthur Conan. *120 Short Stories (Annotated): A Short Stories Collection*. Published on Kindle, 2017.

Gifford, Elisabeth. *Secrets of the Sea House*. New York, N.Y.: St. Martin's Press, 2013.

Hollander, John, Compiler. *American Poetry: The Nineteenth Century*, Volumes I and II. New York, N.Y.: Penguin Books, 1993.

Jeans, Peter D. *Seafaring Lore & Legend*. New York, N.Y.: McGraw-Hill, 2004.

Kolbert, Elizabeth. (2018, October) Scary, Squishy, Brainless, Beautiful. *National Geographic Magazine*, 72-91.

Kunzig, Robert. *Mapping the Deep*. New York, N.Y.: W.W. Norton & Company, 2000.

Masefield, John. *Salt-Water Poems and Ballads*. New York, N.Y.: The MacMillan Company Publishers, 1914.

Masefield, John. *Spunyarn; Sea Poetry and Prose*. London, England: Penguin Group, 2011.

Masefield, John. *The Collected Poems*. London, England: William Heinemann LTD, 1923.

McClatchy, J.D., Editor. *Poems of the Sea*. New York, N.Y.: Alfred A. Knopf, 2001.

Morrow, Sylvia, (2018, June) 20 Things You Didn't Know About Sand. *Discover Magazine*, 74.

Paine, Lincoln. *The Sea & Civilization; A Maritime History of the World*. New York, N.Y.: Vintage Books, 2015.

Tarlach, Gemma. (2019, Jan./Feb.) 20 Things You Didn't Know About the Year in Science. *Discover Magazine*, 98.

Carol Mays enjoys hearing from readers and can be reached through her websites:

www.idyllicproductions.org
www.celestialdreams.net

Other Works by Carol Mays:

Strategies, Poems, & Stories for Holistic Living—
Three genres in one book, on the theme of avoiding
some of society's subtle negative influences and
living a fulfilling life.

Poems of Peace and Renewal—Poems from
various sources on the themes of peace and
renewal.

*Halloween Stories & Games for Mixed-Age
Parties*—A short book that includes fanciful
Halloween stories, with optional sound effects for
audience participation.

Stardust, Shadows, and Secrets—Three genres in
one book, on the theme of creating and enjoying
intrigue and enchantment in life. It includes essays,
poetry, and a novella about a young woman who
finds a mysterious carnival in the woods behind her
house and, through this discovery, ends up accidentally transforming her hometown.

Building a Faith for the Future—A serious, inspiring
book that examines the pros and cons of various
religions and some of the cultural factors which
inhibit spiritual well-being. It presents a new
approach to understanding and living one's faith.

Uplifting Poems—A beautiful and inspiring
compilation of poems by many writers, including

classical, on the subjects of Nature, Connection, Fantasy, Magic, Hope, and Play.

Halloween Enchantment; Haunting Poems and Stories—A collection of poems and stories for all who seek an eerie escape from the mundane.

Carol also collaborated with Richard Bachtold and Nina Andersen on a book entitled:

Mystical Poems by Three Contemporary New England Writers—a beautiful book of inspiring, moving poetry.

Poems of Enchantment—An unusual, enchanting, and relaxing DVD which includes poem narrations, visuals, music, and sound effects.

The above works are available from well-known, online sellers, as well as through local vendors.

40377944R00142

Made in the USA
Middletown, DE
27 March 2019